The Affairs of
BAXIGANJ

SUBHOBROTO MAZUMDER

BlueRose ONE.com
Stories Matter
NewDelhi • London

BLUEROSE PUBLISHERS
India | U.K.

BlueRose ONE.com
Stories Matter
NewDelhi • London

For permissions requests or inquiries regarding this publication, please contact:

BLUEROSE PUBLISHERS
www.BlueRoseONE.com
info@bluerosepublishers.com
+91 8882 898 898
+4407342408967

ISBN: 978-93-6261-190-1

Cover design: Tahira
Typesetting: Tanya Raj Upadhyay

First Edition: July 2024

Prologue

Shubhom: The incident

I had watched Madan Puri's men miss a clear shot of Amitabh Bachchan's head about six times in my life. They missed him again this time as he strode out of the bar to get in his car. Had my boss PK, been in Amitabh's place, and had I taken the shot, I would have emptied all available rounds into him, making his body as porous as a sponge. *Deewar* played on mute on the wide-screen wall-mounted television, and I was probably the only one in the restaurant who was watching it.

There had been live music playing in the restaurant a while ago, and a lady dressed up like Zeenat Aman had been singing Dum Maro Dum on a three-piece orchestra. My friend Rajnish, after eating up most of the food we had ordered, went to dance with the lady and started twisting and rolling on the floor in front of her. The lady wasn't appreciative of his innovative dance moves and abruptly ended her performance, refusing to sing again so long as Rajnish was in the restaurant. Rajnish continued his antics on the floor for some more time, and then, realising that Zeenat Aman wouldn't be singing anymore, he picked himself up and went to argue with the manager for not serving him a beer. Everyone else in the restaurant was busy eating or watching Rajnish dancing and fighting with the manager.

Bunty sat at the corner of the table, drinking coke from the glass in the same way a Bollywood hero drinks single malt whisky. He stared at his glass with brooding eyes, as if he was trying to extricate the meaning of his unremarkable life from within the melting ice cubes dunked in his coke. I decided to stay invisible, hiding from everyone around me, and concentrate on something that would help me detox my mind. My eyes landed on two stylishly dressed girls in caps, wearing knotted shirts and bell bottoms, sitting at the table next to ours and sharing a piece of fish cutlet. I tried to fit the face of Asha Oberoi on one of them but it didn't turn out to be a pretty sight. The other girl caught me staring at her, suddenly started smiling and waving at me. Nobody had ever waved at me in my entire life, and the chances of anyone of sound mind intentionally waving at me in the future had the same probability as India winning the finals of the football World Cup. This was serendipitous for me and I abandoned all thoughts of hiding, stood up to be fully visible, and waved back at her with all the energy I could muster. I would have continued waving at her till kingdom come, but realized that she had been waving at another stylishly dressed boy seated at the table behind me. He waved back at her. None of them seemed to be aware of my presence, so I sat down, dejected, and retreated to my shell of invisibility.

The girls had by then settled down and were engaged in an animated discussion, apparently to resolve some important issue between them. I tried to eavesdrop, and after a few moments of snooping, understood that they were comparing the number of affairs each one of them had in their respective life spans. This discussion went on peacefully for some time but then turned into a major conflict when one of them tried to add the people she had friend-zoned to her list. The other girl vehemently opposed the entry of these candidates and began citing some clause that the guys whom she friend-zone don't count as boyfriends, and hence don't qualify as affairs. The girl who had initiated this conversation tried to reason with her that in both cases the effort and energy expended by her was the same, and hence they needed to be taken into account. Her argument, however, wasn't considered valid by her friend and that left her grossly flustered and dejected. She got super-agitated and jumpy, polished off the entire fish cutlet by herself, and left the restaurant in haste as if to gather a few new boyfriends at the earliest to even her score.

I thought of offering myself to calm her down but then she hadn't even noticed me, and anyway, there was always Asha Oberoi for me. All of a sudden, my mind was hijacked by a creeping thought about whether I had even reached the level of being friend-zoned by Asha Oberoi. It grew on me like an uncontrollable black hole, devouring every bit of happiness around me. It triggered a sensation of being wasted, which morphed into a feeling of vengeance and disgust towards all those who had messed around in my life. I wanted something else to concentrate on. Rajnish was still arguing with the manager like an idiot and *Deewar* was still playing on the television with the exact same sequence of events unfolding for the seventh time. Somebody placed some bottles of beer on our table. Or was it coke? I couldn't recall. I had probably emptied about two of those bottles when everything started to appear hazy and foggy.

I don't remember anything that happened thereafter in the restaurant or how I got back to our apartment on Meghmallar Street. Everything around me felt unreal and out of a dream that I desperately wanted to come out of. The abrupt and irritating ring of the landline shook me out of my trance. It was Bordoloi with his maddeningly irritating voice, "Hello sir, where are you?"

I didn't want to answer any of his questions, but just out of formality, I replied, "At our accommodation. We just returned from dinner."

"Where did you go? "

“I told you; we went out for dinner. At the Grand Hotel.”

“At what time?”

This was getting irritating now, and I was in no state of mind to answer all of his queries. I just wanted him to get lost. So, in the politest way possible, I said, “Bordoloiji, I will talk to you in the office tomorrow.”

I was just about to drop the receiver, cutting him off for the night, when he spoke, “Wait, sir. Our boss’s wife has been shot. Just half an hour ago.”

That woke me up a little.

I couldn’t think of any sort of reply.

“What were you exactly doing an hour ago?” he asked.

My head was throbbing now, and the insides of my mouth felt dry like cotton. I couldn’t recall anything that had happened in the last hour. The time of the incident that Bordoloi kept on repeating, coincided with the exact time I couldn’t remember anything about. And I wasn’t in any state to bother about that.

So, I put the receiver down, not wanting to be disturbed any further. But the phone rang again. I threw it off the hook and went to sleep.

Table of Contents

Shubhom: 20 years ago

I had an incredibly long name and an incredibly large family. From end to end, my name was Subhobroto Dev Raj Mazumder. This was, to a certain extent, a burden for me to carry during my younger days at school. My classmates, who had relatively concise and convenient names like Ravi, Roy, and Sohail Sharma, used to infuse me with an inferiority complex regarding my name and it made me grossly unhappy about my primary identity.

After bearing with this type of nomenclature for six full years of my life, I rebelled. I stopped brushing my teeth and eating my breakfast; I even refused to go to school for three consecutive days. I threatened to continue my rebellion until my name was shortened to a more appropriate and bearable one. That is when I learnt that my aunt, who had some sort of fascination for Dev Anand, had given me my middle name, whereas Raj had been added by my grandfather who wanted my name to bear the aura and majesty of the zamindars whom we had probably descended from. My first name was the courtesy of my mother, whereas my father gave me my surname.

Such a diverse collaboration resulted in this gigantic name. Yet, now I shudder to think that if I had a few more relatives at hand, who had also wanted to contribute something to my name, it would have been quite difficult for me to even remember it fully. On the third day of my rebellion, at dinner time, my wish and my threats were made known to all the members of the family, and their opinions were sought out regarding any change in the status of my name. None of them appeared sympathetic towards me. In fact, my cousin wanted to add the name of her favourite footballer, Pele, to my name as well. The proposal was thankfully rejected as it felt out of sync with the rest of my name. It was after much discussion and coaxing that my aunt agreed to give in and withdraw her part of the contribution from my name. She cited that in these six years of my existence, I had done nothing to make myself as respectable or charming as Dev Anand and that me sharing his name might hurt the latter's publicity. My grandfather, too, had some doubts regarding my being as aristocratic as a zamindar and hence decided to chop the Raj part of it as well. Whatever remained of my name was still a formidable one, but no one wanted to curtail it any further.

Nevertheless, it was decided that my name would be shortened to a new nickname, Shubhom, which would be more commensurate with my size. This, eventually, became my name henceforward, and even after twenty years, continues to stay as my core identity. It is also the recognition of my first and last successful decision and endeavour to do anything positive with my life. Everything thereafter went in an uncontrollable downward spiral, powered by wrong and wayward decisions. Some of them were based on the expectations of the people I valued, and the rest were just misapprehensions or overestimations of situations. All of these landed me in a life where I wanted to add 'loser' as my middle name. I desperately tried to find my childhood self within me–carefree, confident, and somewhat more intelligent than the present me, but he was nowhere to be found.

Shubhom: The day of the incident

A miniature whirlwind in the sun-scorched afternoon picked up the reddish dust and dry leaves and scattered them all around the compound. The entire office was busy picking and accumulating these scattered leaves and fragments of garbage in a corner, only for the wind to disperse them again. Our new boss, who had installed himself in the highest office in the building, and looked every bit like Seth Dharamdayal Teja of *Zanzeer*, was surveying the antics of his men from his glass-walled office. He had declared it to be a cleanliness drive. We began with the office compound, which was already cleaned twice a day by dedicated contractual workers. Two eucalyptus trees were uprooted to make space for everyone and to enhance the camera's visibility. The corpses of the trees were strategically dumped beyond the compound walls so that no part of them would come within any camera angle. Among all this, a motley group of men and women scurried around under the sun, putting all their diligent efforts into cleaning an apparently clean compound as if their entire yearly appraisal depended solely on it; they were aware of the big boss's gaze and the cameraman behind their backs.

I tried to find my friend Bunty in the crazy crowd of cleaners and located him hiding behind a tree, staring at the jungle of sal, palash, and eucalyptus outside the boundary wall. The jungle extended up to the brown hills that marked the horizon and consisted of a fauna mostly comprising of stoned-out druggies and newbie lovers, with sometimes their roles being reversed. Occasionally, a few leopards were spotted in the jungle as well, but they probably found sharing an environment with humans too dangerous and left within a few days.

"What the hell are you doing behind the tree?" I tried to pull Bunty out of his trance. In return, he just showed me half a dozen polythene gloves that were being handed out as part of the cleanliness drive.

"What of them?" I asked.

"How many of them should I wear so I don't leave any fingerprints when I strangle our new boss?"

The new boss had a neck like a hippo and was out of range of Bunty's palm size, but why discourage one's dreams? I assured Bunty that we would get a proper measure of our boss's neck as soon as possible, and then took him to the canteen to bring him out of his trance and back to the real world.

It had been about four months since we had joined Pioneer Minerals and Oil Incorporates—or PMO—as trainees, and three months since our new boss was heli-dropped right in our midst. Our collective curses for our new boss in these last three months were enough to damn his next seventy re-births. Yet, he seemed to have a super strong immunity system, and nothing more than a headache ever bothered him in his current life. Our lives on the other hand had gotten wrecked, turned totally topsy-turvy, and had transformed into a hellish nightmare, all courtesy of the new boss. This nightmarish life repeated itself day after day, and our world collapsed. Other important issues like food, friends, work, dreams, aims, and hopes that used to be of prominence earlier in our lives, took a backseat. Our lives now revolved in a stationary orbit around our office and particularly around our boss. The only things that seemed to come between him and us were the strikes that occurred at regular intervals, closing everything down. These strikes appeared to be more inclined to give people some unscheduled rest rather than to meet any justified cause.

Anyway, it was a Friday; that assured at least two boss-less days to recuperate and replenish ourselves and prepare for another renewed phase of humiliation and grilling in the upcoming week. We returned to our accommodation on Meghmallar Street which we shared with Ramanujam and Rajnish. Ramanujam had recently fled to the jungle for some project to stay beyond the range of PK, dumping his load of office work on us to complete.

Our accommodation was an abandoned chemistry laboratory that had been cleared up to make space for us. However, it still reeked of benzene and the smell pervaded deep inside all of us, reminding us of our hopelessness and miserable life at every moment. Rajnish had returned from some tour and appeared to be in a more pathetic state than any of us. Throughout the week, he had been the protocol officer to some foul-tempered retired vice-president of our company at some conference. He had opted for this trip, assuming that it would be an opportunity to have some fun and hear some lectures about yet-to-be-discovered oil fields in Baxiganj, which everyone kept talking about. But as it turned out, his basic job profile in the tour comprised of escorting the said dignitary to the toilet, getting his dressing gown ironed, paying his bills, and explaining to people that this fellow wasn't actually smoking in a no-smoking zone but was just chewing a pipe that was devoid of any tobacco just to show off his style. He endured this for the first three days of the week and on the evening of the fourth day, he turned up in sunglasses, reporting an attack of severe conjunctivitis.

The retired vice president sent him back from the conference immediately on forced leave.

From then onwards he remained in his room, sulking, trying to figure out whether he should give up his job or tear up his M. Tech certificate. Finding his certificate from within the disorderly dump of his belongings in his room would have required an effort equivalent to unearthing Tutankhamun's tomb. So, he tried the other alternative of writing a resignation letter but found out that he wasn't in a proper mood to write one. He needed something that would help him think straight and feel better to get into the proper groove before penning down his resignation as if the bourgeois poet, Milton, was sitting down to write Paradise Lost. It was in such desperation that Rajnish went out and procured two tablets from somewhere, which he claimed to be LSD–a tool to wipe out every bit of negativity within us instantly and feel good, at least for a while.

The tablets appeared and smelled like normal medicinal tablets, but then Rajnish insisted that he had emptied 80% of our entire monthly dinner budget on them. He handed me a tablet and instructed me to keep it under my tongue. He told me that after a while when the LSD kicks in, my mind will feel lighter and happy thoughts will flood my brain. He put the other one in his mouth as Bunty looked on with the same expression as Ranjit leers at his heroines in his movies.

"Where's mine?" Bunty demanded.

"You don't need one. You can hallucinate on your own. And anyway, we need somebody to watch over us here."

Well, the first part was true. He indeed imagined things and shaped them up in his mind at his convenience. He didn't need anything for that.

"Why is it always Mohd. Rafi for you and Mahendra Kapoor for me?" I couldn't decode what Bunty meant by this; it appeared to be some kind of rhetorical question, so I left it unanswered.

The lights were switched off as we started our experiment with LSD. Nothing happened except several mosquitoes starting a philharmonic orchestra around my ears. A cat howled somewhere as if it was being strangled, and some girl in the neighbourhood began crying, or she could have been singing some sort of classical song. I tried to think of Asha and our fieldwork together in Ghatshila. I remembered the times she sat beside me. The only time she had held my hand was when she was slipping off the top of the dolerite dyke on the banks of the Subarnarekha. The way she had asked me to hold her copies and camera as she measured the rocks with a clinometer was still ingrained in my head. I even conjured up a dream plan, or things I would like to dream about her, but then suddenly she dissolved into oblivion. Then, instead of her, our boss's face, with his snake-like smile, zoomed in before me out of nowhere. Flashbacks of him insulting me, incidents that I had hidden from myself and never wanted to recall again played on sequentially before my eyes. All these could never be categorized as happy feelings that make you feel lighter or more energetic. This was probably some type of antidote to LSD, pushing me into even darker and more depressive feelings.

I peered around in the dark room to figure out how Rajnish was faring with his LSD but he wasn't in the room. I saw his silhouette in the bathroom, spitting out the contents of his mouth in the wash basin.

"This isn't LSD!" I cried out.

"This is Digene, you *ahmmaq*. We were fooled!" Rajnish added.

I had been hallucinating on antacids. No doubt it tasted familiar.

"Now what? I chewed it down."

"Why waste the Digene? Let's go out and eat something."

And so, off we went in search of dinner. The night was moonless, but it was still young. It smelled of wildflowers and mahua blooms. The air around us had something intoxicating in it that made us forget about everything else but ourselves. Everything around us was strangely silent, as if on a pause for something that was about to happen. It was only after dinner, when we returned to our accommodation, that we learnt from Bordoloi that somebody had missed our boss and shot his wife instead.

Rajnish:

The day after the incident

Thriller stuff–what we call *sansani khez* in Urdu–was happening in this sleepy town. Our boss and his wife had been on their way to some party at the office club on their Lambretta scooter around 9 p.m., about the same time we were having our dinner after fooling around with the LSD stuff when somebody had put two 9mm bullets through her. One of those bullets entered her below her right shoulder bone, punctured her right lung, and exited through her back, whereas the other bullet was found lodged near her right lung. The impact of the bullet had thrown her off the scooter and onto the road, where she had collapsed. She was carried off to a hospital in an ambulance and was presently unconscious in an ICU bed.

Our boss was unhurt, but he was in a state of shock. Though a few people were there on the road, none of them had spotted the shooter, who was still absconding. Police had been informed, and they were investigating the issue. They had seized the Lambretta for forensics and were waiting for our boss to regain his bearings so that they could question him. All this information was provided to us by Bordoloi, who in reality, was our office assistant, but considered himself the office centrepiece—our *noor e daftar*. Each part of the information was punctuated by a barrage of queries like where we were at the time of the incident, where we had our dinner, what we had, whether we were drunk, and why it took so long for us to eat. It appeared that he was trying to conduct an investigation himself before the police even initiated theirs. He volunteered the information that he was at a family function and even offered to provide the phone number of his relative for us to check out his alibi as if we cared.

None of us had ever met the boss's wife, but we knew what she was capable of. News permeated from Delhi, where our boss had previously been stationed, that she had invaded his office several times and replaced all the female employees working there. Our boss did put up some form of protest, but those were washed out in the barrage of invective and flowery vocabulary his wife had used there. People from his office, who had visited his home in Delhi, used to tell us that they were forced by her to leave within half an hour, irrespective of their gender, and never dared to return. Colleagues who had their residences near him had reported the couple shouting at each other at unearthly hours. Some even said that the wife had a habit of locking our boss out of their flat at night, and our boss was frequently seen spending the night in his car or his cubicle in the office. I learnt more about her when one odd day, in the office our boss had unexpectedly offered me some *kheer* to eat, which he said his wife had made for us. I was suddenly overwhelmed by his generosity; I felt happy and cared for. But this serendipitous feeling lasted until I placed the first spoonful in my mouth. Whatever it was, that thing tasted more like Mohr's solution that I had accidentally drunk during a titration experiment in the chemistry class in our college. After suffering the torment of going through the entire bowl full of the *Kheer*-like thing under the boss' eagle eyes, I realized that anyone who was compelled to eat this kind of stuff every day would indeed turn into a sadist like him. It was Frankenstein's diet and no lesser person might have a heart strong enough to have it. I also learnt that the boss's lunch regularly goes into the garbage bin along with most of our office work. Bordoloi brought him food from his home. That particular day, the boss's dustbin had been taken out to be emptied, and I was unlucky enough to be substituted for it. Anyway, this was supposed to be kept a secret, so I buried it deep in my heart.

——————————

By the next day, the doctors had removed the bullet from his wife's body, but she was still in a critical condition with her vital parameters not showing any signs of improvement. Meanwhile, the police questioned the boss and learnt that as he was driving down the road, he saw a flash, heard a sound, and then something zipped past his ears. He was too dazed to figure out anything. So, he stopped his scooter and found his wife lying in a pool of blood a few meters back. He panicked and called Bordoloi, who, according to his remaining senses, would have been of maximum assistance in such an emergency. It was Bordoloi who had arranged for an ambulance that took PK and his wife to the hospital. Some people had gathered by that time, but none of them noticed the shooter or had witnessed the actual chronology of events. The shooter had conveniently chosen a dark and empty part of the road for his job. The entire job appeared to have been planned and executed to perfection by some professional who was still at large. The victim of the shoot-out, our boss's wife had an almost non-existent social life and I don't think anybody would ever think of wasting two bullets on her.

There was also a parallel investigation happening at PK's home–an ugly two-story house with a red-walled boundary that PK shared with his wife, mother-in-law, and her dog. The house stood secluded from the others houses in the area because PK's wife didn't like the concept of neighbours. When enquired by the investigating officer, the mother-in-law informed that she did have some premonition that something terrible was about to happen that night. She had heard some loud noises at the back of her house as well as somebody shouting from there, almost about the same time when the incident occurred. The backside of her house was a grassy area that skirted the jungles of sal and mahua visible from our office, and even the druggies avoid the area after sunset. PK's mother-in-law had ventured out on the roof with a torch but hadn't spotted anyone wandering there. All she could see was a dark nightscape, interrupted by howls of jackals. From her experience, it was an eerie situation that was an omen of something evil. She had heard jackals cry behind the farmhouse in Delhi, too, when her daughter had gotten married to PK. She had wanted to warn her daughter about that but there were no means of doing so. When asked if her dog behaved awkwardly at that time, she responded that the dog was trained only to bark at PK. Since he wasn't at home, it had been sleeping peacefully, recharging itself for the time when PK got back. The police searched around for something that would match the mother-in-law's narrative but couldn't find anything definitive. So, they left it to be a figment of an overprotective mother's hyperactive imagination.

This, again, was what Bordoloi told us while enquiring about his doubts between his statements. However, this time, as an afterthought, he added that we were far too clumsy to be called professionals in any sense of the word.

We had been smart when we were recruited four months back. The placement agent from PMO had said that we were the smartest among all the candidates and we had in us what the company desperately needed. That was, however, not true. I had seen Shubhom throughout college, and nobody in the right sense of mind could ever consider him smart. That fellow talked to himself, lived in a time warp, had bouts of memory loss, and even considered Asha Oberoi as his imaginary girlfriend. He had been in love with Asha at IIT since the very first year, but he couldn't ever muster the courage to tell that to her. Finally, on the day of our convocation, when Asha Oberoi walked out of the hall and out of Shubhom's life with her newfound boyfriend, Shubhom declared that he had been cheated on. From that point onwards, Shubhom sought vengeance against Asha Oberoi by gazing at women as if he were trying to destroy their modesty with his eyes. This was one of his many hidden talents that could make him a black-belt-level prodigy among perverts. In either case, he failed to move on from what he called his only love, being completely aware of the fact that he wouldn't ever get her back.

Shubhom seemed like he was born about twenty years later than he was supposed to, straight out of the 1960's. He wore dresses that Shammi Kapoor used to wear in *Teesri Manzil*, walked in an angular gait like Dev Anand did in *Khoya Khoya Chand*, and his favourite music was still 'Come September'. He failed to update himself beyond that and probably even dreamt in Eastman Colour. He thought of himself as an extension of Dev Anand, Shammi Kapoor, Shashi Kapoor, Soumitra Chatterjee, and Joy Mukherjee. And being all those characters, he searched for a girl for himself who'd be a mixture of Asha Parekh, Mumtaz, Mala Sinha, Nanda, and Waheeda Rehman in equal proportions. This was a difficult thing to find in any dimension or any version of the multiverse, but his quest still goes on—his never-ending *justooju*.

Even his moral values and ideologies stayed that way. He believed he was a communist just because he was born in Durgapur in the late seventies when Durgapur was covered entirely in red banners and posters. Durgapur, then, was still a city just born, and a perfect place to grow up as a communist. There, virtually everyone knew Pasternak and Gorky better than our contemporary poets. Whenever anything bad happened in the capitalist world like the Vietnam War or the Iraq Invasions, some citizens of Durgapur would march to the *Lal Maidan* (Red Ground) football field and chant slogans, as if this was the only communist way to set the world back to perfection. Yet for him, it was the most charming city. To emphasize his *fitoor* or obsession with Durgapur-induced communism, he kept a copy of Das Kapital and a Black Book of Linux on his table. However, he never opened either of them. They had remained on his table and had eventually killed a family of rats who came to feed on them. Ramanujam had later wrapped the books in glossy paper and had given them away as a gift at a wedding we gate-crashed.

On the wall behind Shubhom's bed was a black-and-white poster of a white-bearded fellow whom he referred to as Karl Marx, though it could easily pass off as Santa Claus in an evening suit. To further this impression, Shubhom could even rattle off the names of all the Comrade General Secretaries of Soviet Russia in one breath, starting from Stalin, Khrushchev, and Brezhnev to Andropov, Chermenko, and Gorbachev, and yet had a very faint idea about who the Presidents of India were between Dr Radhakrisnan and K.R. Narayanan, filling the gaps of his ignorance with random names. Whenever he was asked to give his opinion on anything, he compulsively added words like revolution and bourgeois to it, which wouldn't have even a remote connection to anything being discussed. That was Shubhom, mostly living, believing, and showing off some sort of *tasawoor-e-aalam*–a make-believe world that lacked any connection with the actual world–in which people like us with goals and dreams would never manage to exist.

Bunty:

A couple of days after the incident

Shubhom was not the nutcase everyone thought he was. He had his dreams, his ambitions, and his little world, but then the person around whom he had built it moved away from him, and his entire world collapsed. From then onwards, he always wore a salesman-type smile, as a defence mechanism to conceal his feelings. He kept that smile on even when our boss threw his files in his face and he had to pick them up one by one from the floor in front of a chuckling Bordoloi. That night, after office, he had declared that our boss had no right to live on this planet anymore. Even then he had his smile on, and as always, nobody was bothered.

Somebody from the police station had called Rajnish and informed him that they would be visiting Sunday morning at around seven to have tea and breakfast with us and to ask us a few questions. I am pretty sure it was Bordoloi who had brought us into this loop and then made us a part of this investigation. Anyway, it didn't matter. What mattered was getting up on a Sunday morning before seven and making tea and breakfast for someone else. This was something I would never do for anyone.

Baxiganj wasn't a big city, just an insignificant small town with most of its people living contently within the sleepy limits of it. It was almost lost in the rocky and rolling lands of the Chhotanagpur plateau that stretched endlessly into the dark green forests of Sal, Mahua, Gulmohar, and the fiery red Palash trees that grew there in abandon. Nobody in its entire history had ever gotten shot. People here were mostly engaged in business, a few people worked in mills, and others worked in their farms. The people manning the police station in Baxiganj spent their time mostly controlling VIP movements or in rare cases, solving theft cases or mediating fights. So, this shootout ranked as a very high-profile case, and as per Bordoloi, somebody had been sent from the district headquarters to investigate the attempted homicide.

The officer came right on time and banged on our door so hard that it jolted us out of our peaceful Sunday morning rest. None of us, however, bothered to venture out from our dreamlands, assuming that the person bothering us would get the hint and leave us alone. That, however, did not happen, and the man turned out to be more persistent than we had expected him to be. Ultimately, it was Rajnish who ran out of patience first. He got up from his bed, and like a professional somnambulist, walked up to the door, opened it, and without even bothering to see who, or what was at the door, retraced his steps back to his bed and immediately fell asleep again. The policeman at the door didn't expect such a lousy welcome. He followed Rajnish in and when he saw him asleep, he made such a ruckus that it chased away all our sleepiness.

"Good morning, everybody. I am Inspector Avinash," he addressed us after ensuring that our morning wouldn't remain good in any way.

As we greeted him back, he ordered us to get him some tea along with something to eat.

He pointed at Shubhom. "You over there, get it." It was an utterly wrong choice. The only thing Shubhom could ever make was half-fried eggs, most of the time the output of which came out as a black burnt smelly mess, that any self-respecting hen would deny laying.

The officer inspected our accommodation, examining every corner of it, and concluded that we were filthy people. He hadn't come across creatures who lived as shabbily as we did; we readily agreed with his observation.

The tea and the fried eggs Shubhom had prepared for him irritated him even further and made him more impatient. He somehow finished his tea, fished out a packet of Charminar from his pocket, tapped and lit one, and then, after taking a long drag, blew out perfect rings of smoke as if it was the only thing he had been practising throughout his training period. Once the rings disappeared, he started his enquiry with, "How many of you live here?"

"Three," Shubhom replied.

"One of us is in the field," Rajnish added.

"Where were you on Friday night between 8 and 10 p.m.?"

This was an expected question but the way he asked it made it seem that Avinash probably already knew the answer. Shubhom answered with whatever he remembered of the evening, censoring out the LSD part of it. Rajnish wanted to add something more to it but by then Avinash had moved on to his next question.

He then began asking about our boss. About how well we knew him, what post he held, and what type of strategic information was he privy to. The questions appeared to be centred more around our boss rather than his wife. He noted down most of our answers with an emotionless face that kept us guessing whether he was satisfied with the answers or not.

The only question that appeared relevant to the incident was who did we think might be the shooter and what might be the motive behind the shooting?

None of us ever thought about that and we couldn't really answer it, so he came back with a different question, "Do you think that the bullet was really meant for the boss's wife or do you think it was targeted towards the boss?"

Again, we had never thought in that direction. There was probably no apparent reason or motive for anyone to shoot the boss's wife, and even we would have happily killed our boss for the way he treated us. That, however, couldn't be reported to the police, so we answered with a maybe.

"So, you say it is probable."

"Maybe."

"Any particular reason for your answer?"

This was a loaded question. Rajnish tackled it with, "A lot of people don't like him."

"And are you among them?"

There was a deadly silence, like the one when Sachin died in *Sholay*. Avinash glared at us with raised eyebrows, his cigarette still hanging from the corner of his mouth, expecting an answer. The answer obviously didn't come so he changed tactics.

"Look, yesterday I had a discussion with Bordoloi and I know how much you love your boss. I am not bothered about that. All I am asking for is any more reasons for anybody else to shoot your boss."

We remained silent, still under the hangover of the previous question. This disappointed the officer, and he rose to leave, but then stopped midway and said, "In case you find anything, call me. In case you don't, you are my next suspects. And better clean your accommodation or next time you will be called to the police station, and I promise you that you won't like it one bit. I need to close this case as soon as possible."

The impact of this cameo visit was so astounding that momentarily it left us standstill and overwhelmed. Rajnish was the first one to shake out of it and he decided that we needed to find out a reason for our boss being shot. But first, we really needed to clean our accommodation.

The cleaning expedition didn't start too well. To begin with, it was a really difficult job to distinguish between what was essential and what was garbage. I was trapped in the indecisiveness of whether to keep an object or throw it away. Most of my belongings were part of this indecisive category which made me run around first throwing my things away and then re-collecting and restoring them.

The worst part of this cleanliness drive was getting Rajnish to clean his room. His room resembled the primordial state of the universe in which everything was in a disorderly way; nobody had any idea what was in there. Nobody ever dared to step inside his room for two reasons—one, there was no place for anyone to set foot in, and secondly, it was dangerous to do so without any protective gear. In case someone with guts of steel does venture into such a hazardous territory and is lucky enough to make his journey back, he would report a red coloured lid-less plastic dustbin and Cindy Crawford in a red swimsuit adorning one of the walls of his room to be cleanest things in his room. The rest of the room with all the rubbish spread around, would serve as an inspiration to any mathematician to re-learn the concept of infinity. But even Rajnish eventually made some serious efforts to clean his room.

Our cleanup operation ended at sundown. As the madness of the day waned, we returned to our ground state, exhausted and deprived of any energy. Shubhom settled down with his harmonica and played what seemed to be the tune of "*Hai Apna Dil*" at a pace equivalent to Ben Johnson sprinting on dope. Rajnish made an inventory of all the things he had lost in the cleanup operation and simultaneously fretted about all the time and energy he would now have to invest in bringing his room back to its primordial state. I had nothing to do, so I sank into my bed and counted the number of rotations the ceiling fan made in one complete minute. Soon I began vegetating, trying to think of alternate reasons to shoot my boss. This brought me back to all the insults I had suffered from him, so I tried to abandon all those thoughts and frantically began to count the rotations of the fan once more. I fell asleep at about 631 rotations, with no dreams or thoughts, and nobody came to wake me up for dinner.

Rajnish:

About 3 days after the incident

Pioneer Minerals and Oil Inc. was an agency set up for geological mapping and to search for non-metallic minerals in different parts of India. A change in company policy based on some consultancy by an American firm made them diversify in oil exploration in various unexplored and under-explored basins of India. This office in Baxiganj was part of its expanding infrastructure set up only a few months earlier to monitor oil exploration in remote parts. Our basic work here was to go to different wells to oversee oil drilling operations, make maps based on data collected from those wells, and propose where exactly we could drill another well with the maximum chance of getting oil. However, none of the wells that were being drilled here showed any commercial output, though weekly messages from headquarters always indicated that a big discovery was just waiting to be drilled. In the conference that I attended, government secretaries, company bosses, and retired experts like the one whom I had dodged, spoke about this big discovery as if it was Alibaba's cave just waiting to be opened–some version of a *tilismi khazana*. When we heard this story of the hidden treasure for the first time, it was my *dil-i-khawaish* to be a part of this discovery. But then, PK joined this office.

Before becoming our boss, PK had been posted at the New Delhi corporate office of PMO, where most of his work involved making animated and colourful presentations on corporate exploration policies. When he wasn't making such animated and colourful presentations, he kept himself busy by sucking up to his boss. It was during one such presentation that he had been asked by the then director of the oil division of PMO, who also happened to be his father-in-law, to choose some men from his group. These people needed to be efficient enough to look after the affairs of a new office that was to be opened in Baxiganj. PK made a list of all his colleagues in his office whom he disliked and wanted to get rid of and sent it to the office of the director. All these men were duly transferred to this office in Baxiganj. It made PK a happier man, getting a smooth and free run in his Delhi office with a monopoly of making presentations, and buttering up his boss with no one else to compete with.

His merry moments in the office continued for two months until he was served a letter which promoted him to Assistant General Manager and ordered him to immediately proceed to Baxiganj and take charge of the new office along with the efficient people he had earlier so generously disposed of from his group. This landed PK in Baxiganj among people who were eagerly waiting to seek their vengeance. For PK, all of his joyous times ended in a flash. Here, in hostile territory, he had no presentations and no boss to butter up. He had no idea of the work he was supposed to do and none of his colleagues, whom he had ditched earlier, helped him in his work.

Within a month of his assuming office, all his erstwhile efficient men got their transfers back to Delhi, where they made themselves busy making animated presentations and buttering up their bosses. PK was grounded, and he desperately tried to reach out to his father-in-law to get him out of Baxiganj. However, the director's office told PK in no uncertain terms that if he wanted to further his career, it would be best for him to remain where he was and stay out of Delhi. PK's father-in-law was a blue-chip level sadist of a much higher calibre than PK, and to further PK's misery he had appointed a general manager above PK who was immune to buttering, and an ever-nagging Lila Chitnis-type mother-in-law in PK's home. Both of them tried their best to ensure that PK didn't find any happiness in his life anymore. To further increase his agony, and simultaneously drive home his feelings towards our boss, his father-in-law gifted a dog to his daughter, who, like everyone, didn't like our boss at all.

It was at this precise juncture that PK became our direct controlling officer and our sectional head in PMO in Baxiganj. Till then, we had somehow assumed that the PowerPoint presentations of the recruitment agent about us being talented were true. However, PK was under the presumption that we were a bunch of clowns who had been explicitly inducted by his father-in-law and sent to this office to amuse him and compensate for the injustice meted out to him. This resulted in a daily exercise of utter humiliation and embarrassment for us in the office. Day by day, the insults piled on and life boiled down to being a burden. After a little while, though, the insults that had earlier penetrated our souls felt a bit more bearable. Our level of tolerance had increased and our self-esteem had dropped to a level so low that we realized there was a dangerously little difference between Bordoloi and us. Nothing we did ever appeased PK, and everything we didn't do made him mad. After a few weeks, we attained enlightenment and understood that the sole meaning of our existence was to get insulted by our boss so that he could feel better about his own humiliations.

Every morning, we were huddled in his room at the behest of a morning meeting that PK chaired with a facial expression loaded with perennial disgust for us. This session became a routine ritual with well-defined clockwork sequences in which he initially humiliated us separately and then cumulatively, using a standard vocabulary of about 500 English words. We were made to realize our collective worthlessness, and any protest or ideas that negated his views were further welcomed by another avalanche of verbal belching that confirmed our worthlessness beyond anyone's doubt. He disapproved of everything about us and throughout the meeting seemed to be engaged in an eternal quest to find something more about us to disapprove of. Sometimes during these sessions, he would call Bordoloi into the room just to rub those insults deeper into our skin, making sure that we would be drained of any quantum of self-respect or *khuddari*. It was like the re-enactment of the bloody battle of Stalingrad, over and over, day after day, every morning, crushing our hopes, expectations, and anything positive within us. Within a few weeks, we realized that all our geological knowledge and the skills that they taught us in Roorkee were of no use to us. The only skill required to survive in this office was to develop an invisible skin as thick and as hard as the hide of all the rhinos of Kaziranga combined.

Ramanujam, our other roommate, thought he was a genius and the only mentally balanced character around in this office. He carried himself like he was the showstopper of every moment he shared with anyone else. Despite that, he fled to the field within two months of the boss's joining, preferring wilderness to this eccentricity. He joined this office with an attitude of a mixture of James Bond and Richard Feynman, probably humankind's last hope for energy security. This feeling made his ego attain escape velocity and soar away to the erstwhile Planet Pluto. His ego was anyway larger than him and could easily curve the space-time fabric of the universe under its weight, leaving very little space for anyone else to fit in. But within a week, PK had shredded his ego to spaghetti and grounded him back on earth to the same depths that he had submerged the rest of us.

Most of Ramanujam's assignments had comprised of making geological maps of an area and getting them finalized by PK. If Ramanujam attempted making any such maps, PK drew an arbitrary line on it, claiming it was a fault and rubbed half of the map away, declaring the map to be bogus. Ramanujam was asked to be more sincere in his duties and redo the map. This, he took as a personal insult to his genius; he repeated the exercise, incorporating PK's lines. But then again, when it was tabled before PK, he rubbed off Ramanujam's faults and the other half of the map, saying it was also bogus.

This went on in an infinite loop, with Ramanujam making maps every day and PK rubbing them off the next day, calling it bogus and proclaiming Ramanujam to be a low-IQ idiot. Ultimately, after two full months of work, Ramanujam realized that he was on the very same assignment which he had begun his career with, drawing meaningless random lines on a paper to make a map that would never be completed. This was when he fled the office to work in the jungle outside the domain of our boss.

There was a strange pattern and style in which PK used to run his office. All the files marked for him never stopped at his table. He sent them round and round, sticking yellow chits on them until the sender got frustrated and recalled the file back. Even a file asking him for a simple geological input was forwarded to Bordoloi for necessary action, who would roam around with it under his armpits for a few days. When he got tired of carrying the same files, he would mark them to the office attendant, Mishraji, who most likely couldn't read. Shubhom would take it from him, try to solve it, and suggest something to the boss as a solution. However, both PK and Bordoloi would ridicule him for this and order him to focus on his matters. His ideas would however be noted in the file and the file would then be sent back for more clarity. If it was returned, it would again retrace its usual locus until it was called back by the frustrated sender. The only file our boss initiated was the request for a microwave oven as an infrastructure for microwave remote sensing, which would help with understanding land subsidence and its relation with oil production in and around Baxiganj. The file made its way to the GM sitting on the floor above us, where it was terminated and returned to our boss. He didn't get the microwave oven to prepare his lunch in the office.

But returning to the current event, the boss's wife had slipped into a coma so the police had no chance of questioning her and reconstructing the situation. They were now of the firm belief, though, that the target of the shooter had been our boss. His wife was just collateral damage. The first shot, fortunately, or unfortunately, missed our boss and hit his wife. Therefore, the second shot was fired, which again missed our boss. Both shots were fired from the same pistol by the same person from the same point. After the second shot, the shooter didn't get time for a third shot since some people had gathered near his target. The point of the shooting was estimated to be the rooftop of an abandoned single-story house fifty metres away. The way the shots had been fired, indicated that the shooter was probably a professional or a contract killer hired by somebody. The police assumed that after he completed his job, he crossed the border and ran off to Nepal. Presently, they were in search of a motive behind someone attempting to shoot our boss and believed that the person who had hired the shooter was still in Baxiganj and would make an attempt on the boss again. Two armed personnel had been hence deputed to guard our boss and follow him wherever he went. In addition, our company has employed security guards to guard our boss's house 24/7. The boss had been asked to make a list of people who could be possible suspects. Last, we heard; he had included us as well as his mother-in-law in that list but had left Bordoloi out of it. The rest of the list was confidential and even beyond the *ilm* of Bordoloi.

Ramanujam:

About 3 days after the incident

It was the best time to be in Baxiganj—just after the rains, with the wind beginning to get its chill again, and the evenings getting fragrant and dewy in a romantic way. A festive hangover lingered in the atmosphere and people went around in their bright and new clothes. Those nincompoops with whom I share my accommodation were probably still fooling around our boss, but at least they have their lives outside the office. Here, I was living in a cold and dark bunkhouse-type cramped up cabin inside the jungle that I had to share with my assistant, who couldn't even comprehend my words. This fieldwork might have saved me from the tyrannical clutches of our new boss, but it had also kept me away from the things that I loved the most in my life—good food and my friends. Originally, I was supposed to stay here for two weeks and then return to Baxiganj. Then our new boss ordered me to continue for one more week, citing the lack of any relievers. But even after another week no one came, and our boss extended my trip to forty-two days. Now, I had deserted any hope of ever going outside this jungle.

Everything I touched here appeared to be coated in a thick layer of moisture—all my shirts, shoes, socks, every damn thing. Each day when I returned to my cabin, I had to spend an entire hour removing leeches the size of my index finger from the rest of my body. They came from everywhere—the grass, the tree tops, the water in the streams, and stuck to me as if they had an infatuation with me. So did the mosquitoes, who had the penetrative power of the gamma rays that got through to your skin even after crossing three layers of clothing. Their buzzing had the same traumatic effect on me as Shubhom's mouth organ did. They denied me a single wink of peaceful sleep. Most of the time I was obsessed with the thought of getting even with our boss. From the deepest depths of this forest, one couldn't even guess what was happening outside the jungle, and no one outside would have any idea of what was going on inside it. The only contact I had with the outside world was through a wireless radio from which I would relay the daily progress report to our Baxiganj base, and my assistant whom I sent to the village outside the jungles for supplies. Most of the time he forgot what he went for and returned loaded with weed and bottles of *hariya*. These kept him busy for most of the day and he remained stoned and incommunicado, probably dreaming of good things in his life and pining for better things outside the jungle. Sometimes during full moon nights, there were sounds of drums, singing, and revelry that floated to us mixed with the sounds of the jungle, making me feel lonelier. Other times, it was just a dull silence or the monotonous sound of the river from where we collected water for all of our needs.

Initially, this job appealed to me as adventurous, much better than sitting in that horrid office, drawing those maps again and again and bickering with those halfwits in our accommodation just to set some things right. However, within a few days, the boredom sunk in and I lost interest in everything—even regular things that I used to do with utmost care like brushing my teeth, bathing, shaving, and wearing clean and ironed clothes.

This limped on until the night I found my wooden cabin shaking violently. I was about to rush out, thinking it was a magnitude eight earthquake—one that would have flattened the entire town of Baxiganj, burying everything and everyone including our office, our boss, and his mother-in-law with it, setting me free to return from my exile—but just when I was about to open the door, my assistant stopped me. The shaking continued for another couple of minutes, but this crazy man held me down for another fifteen minutes. When I finally stepped out of my cabin, expecting everything around me to be obliterated, I found only a few broken branches of trees and some of the sensors uprooted. My assistant pointed towards some disgusting thing on the ground, which looked like elephant dung. It was then I understood that the magnitude 8 earthquake that I thought would end PK was an eight-ton elephant that used our cabin as a scratching pad. If I had stepped out, it might have been the end of me. PK, however, would still be alive with all his weapon-grade sadism. The elephant, relieved of its itches, had vanished for now, but it might return with its friends, inviting them over to have a free back rub against our cabin. I didn't want to be there when that happened and needed to get out of there as soon as possible.

So, the next morning, I damaged all the remaining sensors that were required for my work as well as my radio set in the same way an elephant would have done, sent my assistant home, returned to Baxiganj, and got admitted in an empanelled hospital, feigning all the symptoms that I knew of malaria. For two whole days, I tried to do my best to act like a malaria patient. But then, after two days, the night doctor strictly told me that if they couldn't find anything wrong with me by tomorrow, I would be discharged and would have to leave the hospital and join the office the very next day. I didn't wait to be driven out of the hospital, so I checked out myself and returned to our benzene-smelling accommodation on Meghmallar Street the next day.

When I reached our accommodation, I realized that the cretins had managed to lose the key to the front door of the accommodation, and were using a hack-saw to cut off the lock. Rajnish was doing the hard work of sawing off the lock, with Shubhom hovering behind him and directing him how to use the saw more efficiently for better results. As I stepped into his field view, not realizing that I was cutting off the light, Rajnish looked up with an irritated and sweaty face.

"Look who's back! Even the animals couldn't tolerate his attitude and decided to send him back," he said.

That immediately made me feel defensive and I thought that it called for an immediate and equally snarky retaliation. "Look who's talking. Someone who manages to lose everything, from his girlfriend to the keys to his house."

Rajnish always got touchy when anyone mentioned Sunny. He let the lock go, brandished his saw, and threatened, "Don't you say that again or this hacksaw can do way better things than cutting a lock."

Shubhom stepped in between us and tried to defuse the situation. "Hey, let go." He pushed us away from each other and then looked at me. "You heard about PK's wife?"

I had no interest in PK's wife whatsoever, except that she probably does to PK what PK does to us. "No, what about her?"

"Someone shot her when they were going to a party and she is in the hospital."

"And PK?" I asked with a voice loaded with earnestness.

"Nothing, he still lives on."

"How did it happen?" I wasn't interested anymore and had to muster some visible display of fake concern

"No idea. The shooter must have been a moron. He missed PK."

"No, I mean how did the incident happen?"

"I told you just now, the shooter missed PK. Maybe a lack of practice?" Shubhom shrugged.

"Hey, you dummy," Rajnish interrupted, looking up at Shubhom while still moving his saw vehemently on the shackles. "Ramanujam is asking how PK's wife got shot. Describe it to him."

Shubhom finally got it and went on to narrate everything that had happened in my absence, including Bordoloi's phone call and the visit of Inspector Avinash. He was still going on about how he realized that the fried eggs he cooked for Inspector Avinash were rotten when I stopped him with a thank you and threw the spare key I had in my pocket towards Rajnish. Seeing it, Rajnish got all worked up and he showed his gratitude by showering me with a volley of invectives that are not fit to be repeated here.

During lunch, Rajnish informed me that the police had suddenly gotten an eyewitness who had seen the probable shooter enter the building. The witness had been put before a sketch artist, who, based on the description of the witness, reproduced the face of the probable assassin. Inspector Avinash had shown it to Rajnish and Shubhom in the office to find out if they had seen somebody like that. Shubhom recognized him as Samba from *Sholay* and left Inspector Avinash confused as to whether the witness had seen the assassin, or whether it was a figment of his imagination. Nevertheless, they had circulated the sketches in nearby police stations and those along the border, issuing a general lookout for that type of face. Nobody had reported anything about Samba or any other owner of the face till now.

Well, Shubhom was like that. He dragged everything through his imagination and complicated things. He watched old movies because I think they served as a portal to the past–maybe his childhood–for him. Maybe he wanted to re-take all the decisions that made him such an idiot, or maybe he just wanted another chance to propose to Asha Oberoi. Rajnish appeared to be much more practical and sorted compared to Shubhom. Maybe his father had rubbed off on him. Rajnish's father owned a farmhouse on the outskirts of Delhi that he had turned into a resort. He used to rent out this resort to political parties for the safekeeping of their councillors, MLAs, and MPs, irrespective of their affiliation, after election results were declared, ensuring full secrecy and protection. The demand for this after almost every sort of election was so high that Rajnish's father had to open up a chain of similar resorts in different parts of the country. Each of these resorts ran a full house during election season and needed to be pre-booked at least a year in advance to ensure availability.

Despite being such a practical man, Rajnish's father had gotten duped by an astrologer who had predicted that Rajnish would grow up to be a great scientist. He believed in that bullshit and raised his expectations for his son's future to the level of a Nobel Prize winner even before Rajnish had started going to school. Rajnish however, wasn't burdened by his father's presumptions and soon realized that studying wasn't worth all the effort required. He lazed around in the back benches of his classes, somehow managing to get around the top 15 of his section in each class. His father soon abandoned all his fanciful aspirations for him, just hoping for him to pass out of college or at least get into one. The Nobel committee never found Rajnish's address to request him to collect his award, and nor did any other award committee consider themselves fit to confer him one. Rajnish ultimately became a geologist and managed to complete his M. Tech just to console his father. He had a girlfriend in college, a girl from Lucknow named Sunny, who looked like Gabriela Sabatini, spoke in Urdu when angry, and punched like Mohammed Ali's daughter when she ran out of Urdu words. She realized way sooner than Rajnish's father that Rajnish's laziness outweighed all of his merits and that there wasn't a shred of seriousness in him for anything. We never figured out how serious Rajnish was regarding Sunny, but he did pick up some Urdu words as remnants of that relationship, which he keeps using during his conversations.

That afternoon, we visited the roof of the abandoned building to understand how one could fail to kill our boss even after two attempts. The yellow police ribbons restricting people from venturing inside had been removed. The forensics had been completed and whatever information the police could have gathered from the scene had already been collected. The staircase that used to lead to the roof of the building had been damaged and had developed its own ecosystem, comprising various kinds of plants and algae. Even in the late afternoon, it took us some effort to reach the roof and find the position from where the shot might have been taken. The shooter must have done some amount of reconnaissance before the incident. That is, he must have visited this abandoned building quite a few times before finalizing that particular spot for taking the shot because there was only one such spot on the entire roof from where the shooter could have taken the shot at such an angle. Yet, even after such R&D he missed the boss, and we would have to go to the office again tomorrow.

The next day, our boss appeared to be a little mellowed down under the weight of everything that had been happening around him. We were all called into his office and were ready for another salvo of endless insults, most of which would reiterate the obvious facts about how stupid and undeserving we were. Today, however, the conversation veered off on a different track. It was focused on the fact that he was not a coward and would be happy to die for the cause of this company. He even tried a quote from Julius Caesar but then his phone rang and interrupted him. Somebody had redirected a call for the canteen to his office, and the person on the other side asked if there was butter toast for breakfast. He put the phone down and began with Julius Ceaser again when the phone rang once more and this time the caller wanted to add a cup of tea with his butter toast. He cut the call and invoked Julius Ceaser for the third time but forgot it midway and left it hanging in between, searching for words to complete it, and finally availing Lord Tennyson to finish it off. PK waited for the impact of his words to sink in, but not finding an appropriate response from us said that there were people from competing industries who were trying to sabotage the operations of PMO. The attack upon him was a part of that, but he would stand as a rock, taking every blow on him to protect this company. At the end of his lecture, he added that he wanted all of us to have this feeling of selflessness on our part and be like him. Bordoloi repeated every word the boss had said in the third person, and we nodded after every sentence of his as if he was conducting some kind of *satsang*.

Shubhom appeared lost, probably visualising the boss as Jawaharlal Nehru, delivering his tryst with destiny speech, or Ameen Sayani, hosting Binaca Geetmala. I felt like killing the fellow who had missed killing our boss.

Bordoloi suddenly raised his hand as if he had an important point to make.

PK allowed him with a wave of his hand as if he was *Zille-e-Elahi* allowing his court poet Abdur Rahim Khan-i-Khana to compose one more eulogy for him. However, Bordoloi came up with something quite different.

"Sir, if we can conduct a séance, we can find out who tried to kill you."

"How exactly will you do that?" Rajnish asked on behalf of PK as PK stared at Bordoloi with an open mouth wide enough for an AN-32 aircraft to easily fly through.

"We can use someone as a medium and call a soul or a spirit. I know somebody who does that."

"And whose soul or spirit will you call, Bordoloiji?" Rajnish egged Bordoloi further.

"Well, we can call on Madam," Bordoloi looked at PK, scratching his semi-bald head, triggering a cascade of dandruff on his blazer, and went on, "She might have seen who tried to kill you."

"Stop this nonsense." PK suddenly wasn't in a poetic mood anymore, his face turning a shade blacker.

"But Bordoloiji, madam hasn't turned into a soul or spirit yet," Rajnish reminded Bordoloi with his characteristic lack of sensitivity. The room suddenly turned silent and PK's face darkened further.

Bordoloi was visibly embarrassed at this slip-up, but in an attempt for immediate damage control, said, "We can call the spirit of a famous private detective."

"Someone like Poirot?" Shubhom asked.

"Is he dead yet?" Bordoloi wanted to make sure that he didn't get trapped again. "We can ask him to find out who tried to shoot our boss and er... shot madam.".

PK was gazing at Rajnish, Shubhom, and Bordoloi alternatively as if following volleys in the Wimbledon singles match between Boris Becker and Ivan Lendl, and all of a sudden stood up. He stood there for a few seconds, and then with a voice shrill enough to fracture plexiglass, screamed, "All of you, leave my room immediately." I failed to figure out whether he was disturbed by the stupidity of everything or the fact that somebody was attempting to find out who tried to shoot him. I was the last to exit his room trying to slip out un-noticed, but he looked up at me at that precise moment and out of some misplaced feeling of vengeance shouted, "You, there smart-ass. Submit your report and finish up the maps you were working on."

All of a sudden, the jungles of sal and palash, visible through the bay window behind PK with all their wilderness, appeared much more lucrative than the office.

Rajnish:
About a week after the incident

Ramanujam had prepared his field report with the same amount of diligence with which he would have written his dissertation, and going by the size of it, I could safely predict that PK would never even bother to go from one end of it to the other. Yet the sheer amount of effort Ramanujam had put into it would have made my father proud had I ever done that. Ramanujam's father was a renowned professor in quantum physics and for whatever reasons best known to him, named his son after the math genius. Unlike Shubhom, Ramanujam couldn't get rid of his name and it stuck with him with all the dead-weight of expectations associated with it. On top of that, Ramanujam's father got too involved in his teaching and research to care whether Ramanujam was living up to his name.

Ramanujam grew up as a lonely and ignored child, and just to get his father's attention, took upon himself the stress of reaching the same stature as him. It worked to some extent and he remained a topper in every class up until tenth standard. This raised the hopes of people around him, and they started comparing him to his father, and even predicting whether he would be going to MIT, Princeton, or CERN for his higher studies. Then, something happened. Like every normal person, Ramanujam fell in love with one of his classmates, and that, according to him, surpassed all the pressure of academic performance that he had imposed on himself. Things slipped and he barely managed to get a first division in twelfth standard. The worst thing was that in the same year, his father was shortlisted for the prestigious Dirac medal and took no notice of his son's poor performance. Ramnujam faltered and couldn't qualify for any of the entrance exams he had sat for. He blamed all of that on his love affair, broke up with the lady, and vowed never to fall in love again. He got admitted to B.Sc. Geology studied like a man possessed, and subsequently got a lateral entry into an IIT to complete his M. Tech, topping his class with a gold medal. He decided to let go of his ambitions of being like his father and joined Pioneer about three months ago. Those who have known him before say that he has transformed from a simple and cheerful kid to a sophisticated, selfish, snobbish, and arrogant person who easily gets irritated and flies into a rage at almost everything. I think he uses that as an armour to maintain distance from others. Anyway, Pioneer recruited all of us and brought us together, people they consider are specifically required for the immediate future of the company with a common trait—all of us being unlucky in love.

When Ramanujam submitted his 85-page *Materia Medica-sized* report, there were still some vestiges of the morning events from PK's office hanging in the air. PK had been sitting alone in his office with the look of a person suffering from severe constipation. This look intensified when he saw the size of the report and realized that he would need to go through it. He opened the report from its back cover and saw his name in the 'acknowledgement' section, which helped loosen some of his facial muscles and a faint smile formed on his face. Ramanujam had recommended that PK visit the cabin in the jungle and stay there for a night to assess the damage to the sensors. PK removed his name and replaced it with that of the GM sitting above him, changed the elephant attack to unknown circumstances, and sent it to the GM's office citing sabotage from competing industries.

I was stuck at the "competing industries" segment of our boss's noting. Which competitor would be so benevolent as to help us get rid of our company's most non-performing asset? The answer to that was found in the GM's office.

Our boss, though a 24-carat *Qabil-e-qadr* idiot, was also the custodian of all the data sets of the area of survey under his office by virtue of his position. Two of the data sets he owned were a vintage 2D seismic survey of Tandwa and a geochemical map prepared for the same area. Both these data sets were top-level classified data and indicated several prospective zones for gas exploration in the area. However, the exploration block adjacent to this area will be opened up for bidding in a few months. This block was owned by a company called PetroIndia Inc., chaired by someone named Raman. Raman was a batch mate of our boss, who had resigned from Pioneer and had an idea about these datasets. He had tried to get access to these maps and datasets through our boss. He had even tried offering PK a top position in his company and some substantial monetary benefits. Yet, our boss was either too sincere or too scared to get lured by his friend and hand over the data. As the dates of the bidding drew near, Raman had gotten desperate. He had tried to remove our boss from his position through political back channels, but that did not materialize.

On the off chance that he had been successful in removing our boss, Raman had already planned to make somebody, who would be easy to manipulate, the custodian of the data. The attempt to shoot down our boss was probably a part of that desperate plan. Apart from this attack, our boss had reported several attempts by goons hired by PetroIndia to sabotage the operations of PMO, so that Pioneer Oil was forced to vacate and the entire area would become a part of PetroIndia's acreages. There was, however, no evidence against these goons since, after sabotaging, they reportedly crossed the border to Nepal, where they were beyond the reach of Indian law enforcement.

As we exited the executive assistant's cabin with this information, we found Shubhom ogling at the telephone operator who had joined the office a few days back, with his trademark predatory gaze. The telephone operator, however, appeared oblivious to anything and went on to do her work with the serenity of Wordsworth's highland lass in Solitary Reaper. Now, whatever I know of Shubhom, he was probably hallucinating, replacing the telephone operator with somebody more desirable, who would suit his rotten senses in his walnut-sized brain. Shubhom continued with his open-mouthed staring for quite some time, until the lady commented to no one in particular that "staring at a lady for more than 30 seconds can be punishable under the Indian Penal Code." I wasn't aware of any such law but thought that it was best to leave without bringing any more attention to Shubhom. Ramanujam was more prudent and dragged Shubhom out of the hallway and out of any angle from which he could stare at the lady.

As we were leaving, we got called by Mishraji to the corner of the office that he considered his territory. We found him sprawled out on his chair, striving to search for a position which would be comfortable enough to let him doze off when required. When he saw us entering the office, he made a laborious effort to sit up and search for something to do on his table. There was nothing on it except a freshly emptied lunch box. So, realizing the futility of his efforts, he abandoned his charade to look busy and returned to his previous semi-horizontal posture. As we stepped up to his table, he pointed towards Shubhom and, in his trademark nasal tone laden with a heavy dose of warning, cautioned him, "Barkhuddar, you are playing with fire. Stay away from her."

Shubhom stayed silent and didn't bother to answer him, so I volunteered. "Why, what happened?"

"You just listen to me. Stop fooling around with her."

Shubhom got irritated. "Is she related to you?"

"No, sir. Just consider this as an advice from your elder brother. Firstly, she is at least three years older than you." Shubhom shrugged his shoulders, indicating that he didn't care about such statistics.

Mishraji stared blankly at Shubhom for a moment, sighed, and continued, "And secondly, and more importantly, your boss, PK...how shall I put it? He has developed a soft corner for her. I hope you are getting what I mean."

Shubhom froze into a statue at this bit of news, all the reckless effervescence draining from his eyes and turning him into a poster boy of despair.

Mishraji had been expecting such a reaction and hammered in his point. "So, it would be in your best interest not to venture in that direction especially during your probation."

Shubhom nodded, but he didn't seem to hear anything.

Mishraji sank in his chair a bit more and continued, "I am relaying all this to you with the permission of the competent authority."

So that is what this was–an indirect message from PK delivered through Mishraji, warning us not to trespass into PK's domain.

As the day waned and the sun went down beyond the red dust plains that extended beyond Subarnarekha, we lazed around in our accommodation, doing mundane things to wear off our office stress. Ramanujam was jittery throughout the day after what had happened in the office, taking out his anger on the chicken he was trying to cook. He suddenly turned towards Shubhom and asked in an irritated tone, "What was that about?"

Shubhom was washing the dishes and rubbing them dry with the intensity and fervour of Pablo Picasso drawing the Guernica. As expected, he missed the context of the question. "What?" he asked innocently.

Ramanujam got even more livid, his patience crossing its yield point. "Stop rubbing those dishes so hard. No genie is gonna come out of them. Just tell me why the hell were you staring at that telephone operator," he burst out, being more specific this time.

Shubhom left his plates and turned around to explain. "Her name is also Asha. Asha Chatterjee."

"So?" Ramanujam didn't understand.

"The way she sat on the table, fiddling with the pencil, she looked exactly like Asha Oberoi."

Ramanujam turned towards me. "Is that so?"

I was trying to cut an onion for the salad and keep my tears from blocking my vision. I had no idea how Asha Oberoi looked while fiddling with her pencil. So, I just pursed my lips and shook my head in a no.

Ramanujam turned towards Shubhom.

"She has a mole on her nose on the exact same spot that Asha Oberoi had. She even wore the same perfume. Didn't you notice?" Shubhom defended himself further.

"So what? Why were you staring at her like you wanted to burn a hole through her?" Ramanujam still couldn't get the point.

"Well, I fell in love with her and I wanted her to acknowledge that." Ramanujam got agitated and was on the verge of erupting and exploding like Mount Vesuvius when a burning smell coming from the cooker filled our kitchen and put an end to the volcano. There went our dinner. Now we'd have to eat out again. The chicken he was cooking probably won't be recognisable without a proper post-mortem. Ramanujam kept the pressure cooker aside with its lid on, lacking the courage to explore what lay beneath the lid.

"Why don't you throw it away?" I asked

"Throw what? He is too heavy?" Ramanujam looked at Shubhom, still mad at him.

"Throw whatever is in that cooker instead of covering it up." I elaborated.

"Nope. Until I open the lid, we can still consider a 50% probability of it being edible. It exists in an indeterminate state until then. Let it be like that," Ramanujam tried to explain.

"You don't need quantum theory to cook chicken or to cover up your faults," I tried to reason with him.

"Well, the smell tells us how good it is cooked." Shubhom punctured Ramanujam's theory as well as ego.

Ramanujam turned red and marched out of the kitchen, going into his room to do some yoga or breathing exercises and regaining his composure. He returned to the kitchen after a minute and said to Shubhom, "Well, the next time you fall in love, warn us beforehand so that we can escape." He turned to me. "And you, don't ever try to teach me quantum theory."

I still don't know what Shubhom made of that but he kept on mumbling something to himself as we got ready to go out to dinner. I wanted to ask him if he really thought he was in love with her, but he didn't seem to be in the mood or the condition to answer.

Bunty:

About a week after the incident

Each time Shubhom tries to move on ahead in his life, something invariably happens that dismantles all of his plans, dragging down his confidence to sub-zero levels. After every such incident, he behaves strangely and starts doing odd things. I have known Shubhom since he was a child and have witnessed many instances of such behaviour. Sometimes, when he loses his bearings and starts acting awkwardly, I try to take over and manage things so that Shubhom doesn't look like a fool. So that is why when Mishraji deflated Shubhom's ballooning feelings for Asha Chatterjee, I was apprehensive about Shubhom's reactions. But this time, things didn't appear bad enough for me to take over.

Shubhom was born in a house filled with people ready to take care of him. That probably led to the development of his perpetual hunger for affection. This trait had gotten strengthened over time to the extent that he expected affection from everyone, and considered a lack of affection as rejection. When he left home for college, the familiar surroundings changed and he became a shy, cold, and needy fellow, fearful of getting rejected over and over. He began to spend his time confined alone or restricted within a small group of people who he thought accommodated his feelings. He began to classify people around him based on their expressed affection–those who were his friends and showed him affection, and people whom he thought rejected him and were his potential enemies.

When PK joined this office, Shubhom was assigned to assist him with his technical work. That also included everything nontechnical and menial like booting his desktop, xeroxing his papers, receiving his phone calls, emailing his documents, and finally, switching the lights, fan, and AC of his room on and off when he stepped in and out of his haloed chamber. PK considered this as giving us exposure to the basics of office work, without which we could never become good executives, and for which we should be immensely grateful to him. Shubhom somehow believed him and did all those jobs with utmost honesty. But inspite of all his sincerity in providing his supra technical assistance, Shubhom was verbally butchered almost every single day in the morning meetings for performing below the expectations of PK. These, too, were requirements for

Shubhom to transform him into an efficient executive. PK made sure to convey to Shubhom that he felt really bad during these sessions, yet he had to do all this because he genuinely cared for Shubhom and wanted to see him as a successful manager one day. Bordoloi was a permanent fixture in all of those meetings, adding his comments about feeling bad as well, but that he, too, wanted Shubhom to be as successful as PK. Shubhom listened to all of it with a nonchalant face, with a precursor of a smile stretched between his lips.

When we joined this office, they conducted a psychometric test on all of us, the results of which were kept confidential in our personal files. We never got to know how we were evaluated, but PK probably had access to all that data and knew all of our strengths and weaknesses, which he used in formulating separate strategies to deal with each of us. I am pretty sure that Shubhom was being handled by one such strategy, which PK used on him almost every day to make him do his bogus work without any type of protest. I realized that after a few of these morning sessions and tried to warn Shubhom about it, but he was either too much of a dumbass or loved being made mincemeat every day. Sometimes, the way PK and Bordoloi treated Shubhom would breach even my tolerance levels and a desperation to do something to stop all this would creep into me. I, however, controlled myself, trying not to do anything that would precipitate the situation into some sort of flashpoint.

On that hope-filled and fun-laden evening when we had gone out for dinner and on returning learnt that some imbecile had attempted to shoot PK, missed him, and instead sent his wife to the hospital, Shubhom had walked out of the restaurant midway through Rajnish's fight with the manager. He was probably hallucinating about PK, hatched some ideas in between, walked out when all eyes were on Rajnish, and then claimed that he couldn't remember where he went. I followed him for a while to drag him back but then left him alone. He returned to our accommodation just when the phone rang, and Bordoloi broke the news that somebody had attempted and missed to kill our boss. When inspector Avinash came to interrogate us a couple of days later, Shubhom conveniently left this part out of his version, and Rajnish, for some strange reason, chose to stay quiet at that moment, fussing more about why his tea smelt of kerosene.

Rajnish has this odd habit of behaving unpredictably during serious circumstances which he attributed to his inherent confidence in handling situations. At times, his confidence gravitated to overconfidence and made a mess of everything. Yet, irritatingly, he still doesn't acknowledge this as a failure and keeps on repeating this randomly. This time, he had suddenly acquired sleuthing instincts, trying to find who had tried to shoot our boss, poking probing questions at everyone, as if Inspector Avinash had personally delegated this job to him. He even relayed all the information that he had gathered from the executive assistant of the GM to Inspector Avinash sincerely, but the Inspector already knew it and told him that he needed to search more.

That evening, Inspector Avinash visited us again. This time taking no risk of food, he carried a packet of samosas with him. As Rajnish relayed the day's events to him, Avinash informed us that Raman had been in Baxiganj on the night of the shooting. He had been staying at the Hotel Shahjahan Regency and had returned to his office in Delhi two days after that. At the time of the incident, he had been at the bar of the hotel, drinking with a friend of his, after which he had his dinner and went to sleep. The hotel staff had confirmed this so he couldn't have been at the place of the incident. Nevertheless, there remained the possibility that Raman had hired someone else to shoot our boss and then arranged for him to escape to Nepal. However, Raman had not recognized or declined to recognize the face of the shooter who resembled Samba of *Sholay* and he had also denied any involvement in the incident. His dealings with any executive of Pioneer were purely business-oriented, based on mutual understanding, and there wasn't any sort of hidden agenda behind them. However, Baxiganj police still suspected Raman to be the main culprit behind the shooting, so they have been keeping track of his activities and trying to derive any clues that would point to him as the culprit. However, so far, that has been a hopeless venture.

So, the next suspect was the person who would have replaced our boss in case everything had gone in order. This man could have handed over the concerned maps to Raman when he would have become in charge of this office. Our help was specifically required to find that person out as soon as possible.

While leaving, Inspector Avinash informed us that PK had planned to announce a cash reward for the people who would help to nab the assassin or provide adequate information to get him arrested.

That implied, that PK, despite invoking Julius Caesar and Tennyson to project his bravura, was timid and needed a bounty hunter to protect him from getting assassinated. Also, instead of PK scaring the hell out of us every day, we could now do that to him.

Shubhom:

About a week after the incident

Since the telephone operator's name was Asha Chatterjee, Rajnish and Ramanujam had started calling me Lady Chatterjee's Lover. Asha Chatterjee was older than Asha Oberoi and didn't seem to be interested in me too much. However, the way she sat while working reminded me of Asha Oberoi, and I fell for that. My heart started fluttering like a dancing Shammi Kapoor, and everything around me smelled like Arsalan's biryani. The same thing had happened when Asha Oberoi had stepped into my birthday party in Laguna in Roorkee, dressed in that elegant blue saree and high heels. I had forgotten everything that had happened after that moment until Rajnish and Sunny had collected me from the banks of the Ganga Canal, about a mile away from Laguna. I had walked out of my birthday party, and the people I had invited were searching for me to pay the bill to the restaurant.

Asha Chatterjee joined this company around the same time as we did. She had been posted in the Civil section initially as an office attendant, until one day our boss visited that section, saw her, and decided that she would be of more use in his office. He initiated the transfer procedure and the girl who was earlier managing file distribution became the girl who now connected telephone wires to direct calls. There wasn't any space in our boss's cabin and the corner outside the boss's chamber was taken up by Mishraji, so the boss parked her upstairs where she kept herself busy managing calls and noting something or the other down in her register.

Mishraji had gotten hold of some more information about Asha that he had gleaned from his discussions within his friend circle. She had completed her post-graduation in history and was previously engaged to one of her classmates from college. She used to do small roles in theatres with him after her classes. However, her fiancé had ditched her and she had joined this office, simultaneously preparing for state civil services and bank jobs. If any of her plans didn't work out, PK had promised her a posting in the most lucrative Establishment Section of HR, and now she was just waiting to get there. The fact that PK didn't have the power to sanction such transfers was a different issue altogether, but Asha Chatterjee had no idea about that. All of PK's promises to her were duly backed up by assurances from Bordoloi, who kept on asserting that PK had already made arrangements for her transfer and an official order was on the way.

Bunty had advised me to gift her something and write her a letter so that she could be aware of my feelings. However, with the overpowering presence of PK and his promises and assurances, there was very little chance of any of my feelings getting acknowledged by her. So, until and unless PK was removed from our midst, it would be a rerun of the Asha Oberoi episode all over again. That's why Bunty decided to help me form a plan to get rid of him. We decided to steal and hide those classified maps that Rajnish had told us PK was custodian of. If they were missing, PK would be held responsible for it. He would be given a deadline and would spend his time searching for them but would never find them. Ultimately an enquiry or an investigation would be set up that would result in PK's suspension or may be his transfer from this office. With PK gone, none of his assurances would mean anything to Asha Chatterjee. That would be my best chance to talk to her, to express my feelings, and even propose to her. In any case, if things turn awry, we could always put those maps back in the place where they belonged. We figured that those maps were probably in the steel cupboard in PK's office where all the official documents were kept. Its keys were usually in the first drawer of our boss's desk; I had seen him open it a few times.

There were still multiple security levels before one could reach those maps, though. We knew that Rajnish and Ramanujam would never agree to do this, so the first job was to keep them out of the loop and send them somewhere so they wouldn't be anywhere near the scene of the activity. Next, Bordoloi had to be taken care of so that he wouldn't mess around in the office. He probably still held a degree of suspicion that we had something to do with the attempt on our boss and that is why he still tailed us around in the office. Most importantly, all of this had to be carried out when the boss was out of the office complex. And even if all the above conditions were successfully met, there was still Mishraji in his station outside the boss's office. The cabin door had a glass porthole and everything that happened inside it was like a Bollywood thriller to him. Mishraji was old with his son approaching retirement. He was also hard of hearing and used hearing aids that were sensitive enough to automatically stop working whenever he was asked to do some work. However, the best and the most predictable thing about him was that he spent most of his time in the office, sleeping on his chair. So obviously we decided to execute our operation when Mishraji was asleep.

In conclusion, we would have to execute our plan when Bordoloi was nowhere near us, our boss was out of our office complex, Rajnish and Ramanujam were busy somewhere else, and Mishraji was asleep. The total window of opportunity would be around seven minutes, and within that time we were to search for the key to the cupboard, open it, search for the maps, take them, hide them somewhere in our jackets, close the cupboard, keep the key in its place, and then exit the cabin.

The next day, when the boss went to the hospital to take care of his wife who was still in a coma, I planned a Mughlai lunch for all of us staying at the 10, Meghmallar Street in the restaurant of the Blue Diamond Hotel, and then dropped out of the plan at the last moment citing an upset stomach. None of them appeared to believe me, but a booking at the Blue Diamond restaurant was too difficult to get, and lunch there was too lucrative to miss, so they left me a few tablets of Digene, wished me well, and went for lunch.

Bunty stayed back along with me as part of our plan. As for Bordoloi, I had planned to send him to the farthest end of the campus to collect some well logs from there. Bordoloi happily agreed to that as most of his friends were posted there and he collected his daily dose of gossip from them. He almost jumped up to go, went to the exit, halted for a moment, returned to his desk and stood there scratching whatever hair remained on his head. That almost stopped my heart, and for one plank-second I felt that it was probably the end of everything I had ever planned in life. However, Bordoloi stopped his scratching, picked up an arbitrary file from his table, tucked it under his armpits, and then left the office with an ear-to-ear smile.

Mishraji, on the other hand, couldn't be sent anywhere and had an unpredictable rhythm of sleep. It was difficult to understand when he was awake and when he fell asleep. We waited for Mishraji to have his lunch. After that, he busied himself with ruminating and picking his nose, checking the output, and arranging them on his table. This went on for about half an hour until his nose ran out of stuff to dig and he got bored and finally fell asleep. Both Bunty and I checked on him to make sure that his snores followed a pattern and were steady. That is when we initiated our operation to get those maps.

The boss's room was unlocked and we tiptoed into his room without disturbing Mishraji. We found the key in his drawer as expected. The only problem was that it was part of a bunch, which meant that we would have to try several iterations before we could open the cupboard. There were six similar keys in that bunch, and the last one of them opened the cupboard with a sound similar to what Bruce Lee makes before kicking someone. Mishraji didn't appear to be disturbed by any of the sounds we made and continued with his snoring. The cupboard had about four racks, and all of them were filled with stacks of various documents and files. It was quite dark with curtains drawn on the bay window, and we were having trouble fishing around in the cupboard for the required data sets.

It took some time for our eyes to adjust, and even then, it was after multiple attempts that we recovered a box file marked "extremely classified". The subject line, which we could barely make out in the dark, read: Seismic and Geochemical Maps of Tandwa. It was the file on which the life and career of our boss depended. We opened and peered into it in the semi-darkness of the curtained room. The file was empty; nothing existed within its covers. Not a single piece of paper. We searched the entire cupboard for anything that looked like a map, but there was no map anywhere in it. However, tucked behind the documents, we found a cardboard box that seemed like it was deliberately hidden from sight. We brought it out and pulled out its contents, hoping for them to be the maps we were looking for. They were not. Instead, arranged inside the box were a few photographs of Asha Chatterjee and one of the scarves she used to wear in the office.

We left it all there, set everything back, and left. But I couldn't think straight for the rest of the day. I talked to Bunty about it and he suggested that we find out more about PK. So, that evening, we borrowed Ramanujam's car to tail our boss's car. Ramanujam's car was an alter-ego of Ramanujam himself and needed loads and loads of attention to do any job. It had its own mind and its own tantrums; it broke down now and then just to garner some attention for itself. This time, however, it behaved properly and reached Hotel Shahjahan Regency without disturbing us. We followed our boss until he reached room 502. He didn't knock and went directly inside clicking the door shut behind him, implying that the person inside was already expecting him.

We returned to the reception and found the manager, a man in his mid-thirties, dressed in a Muqaddar ka Sikandar type jacket with a hardbound standard-sized guest register laid open before him. He seemed completely engrossed in a Jackie Chan movie running on a portable TV before him and I had to ring the bell on his desk twice to bring him out of his Jackie Chan universe. As he peered straight at me through his half-moon glasses, I hurriedly put forward the question that was racking my head even though I knew what the answer was going to be.

"We want to know who is staying in room number 502, It's Asha Chatterjee, isn't it?"

The manager appeared to be a bit low on IQ and was caught on the wrong end of the question.

"We, what's we?"

"Forget about us, is Asha Chatterjee in room no. 502?".

The manager stared at us for a moment as if he had just seen Spock from Star Trek teleport himself in the lobby before him. I had to ring the bell again to help him regain his composure. He again peered at me with his beady eyes behind half-moons and gave a standard answer in a slow and faltering tone,

"We can't provide details of any of our guests in this hotel."

"Its...Its... urgent, we need your help", I pressed on

"The manager somehow wasn't getting focussed on the issue. He was scanning the back of the lobby behind us where posters of sunset in Subarnarekha in Ghatsila were boarded up. I tried to follow his gaze into Ghatsila when he gave us another standard reply, this time slamming the guest register shut.

"It's against company policy, I can't"

This time Bunty pulled out a fifty rupees note from his wallet and slipped it under the manager's out-stretched palm resting on the sun-mica-covered table top.

"Maybe we can suspend this policy for five minutes."

The manager's palm fisted up on the note and he muttered something like "Excuse me, I have some urgent work to do." and vanished in the antechamber behind his desk.

Bunty ran to the table, opened the Guest Register and fervently began to scan the pages till he found what we were looking for.

There wasn't any Asha Chatterjee staying at this hotel. Room 502 has been booked under the name of Mr. Raman.

Ramanujam: Second day of the week after the incident

I had to shield Shubhom the next day by lying to our boss that the nincompoop was with us having lunch at Hotel Blue Diamond. Boss suspected that somebody was in his room rummaging his things in his drawer and cupboard, though everything in them was accounted for. Mishraji swore that he didn't fall asleep in the office, and no human entered the boss's cabin under his watch. Apparently, this affair would have ended there but then Bordoloi entered the scene with his well logs that he had been asked to fetch from the Logging Section. He had forgotten the name of the well for which he had to fetch the logs and had instead brought another arbitrary set of logs for a well whose name he couldn't remember right now. However, despite all this, Bordoloi did remember that Shubhom had sent him to the Logging Section and was probably there in the office even after we had left for our Blue

Diamond lunch. This info led to our boss suddenly getting into silent mode and simultaneously chewing on the fingernails of his right hand. Soon he realized that there was not much left there to chew on and terminated the session dismissing us outrightly from his room. This was followed by a closed-door extra-long animated discussion with Bordoloi where Bordoloi could be seen shaking his head in a dangerous frequency in sync with whatever the boss was saying. Shubhom returned to his cubicle and for some unknown reason started talking to himself mumbling something about Bordoloi. None of that made any sense to me but then as far as we know him all weird things are perfectly normal for him, so we left him alone at peace with his world.

Nothing more happened in the office that day. The boss behaved as he always did-playing somebody terribly busy to indulge in any sort of technical or administrative office work. Bordoloi sleuthed around trying his best to gather data on Shubhom from us and noting them down on his armpit file before finally declaring that Shubhom was a crazy lunatic psychopath. Shubhom stayed grounded in his cubicle preparing a report for yet another well that had gone dry without any hydrocarbon shows. Till now all wells in this area had gone dry and Shubhom had been given the unenvious task of finding out separate reasons for each of them going dry and then suggesting how these dry wells serve as leads for more wells being drilled. Rajnish once advised him to put a disclaimer before his reports that would say "Everything mentioned in the report is fictitious and a figment of the author's imagination. The author assumes no responsibility for the correctness, completeness or quality of the information provided. Any resemblance to the facts and figures or actual events is purely coincidental". In between all this Mishraji moved from his seat, came to Shubhom's cubicle and informed us that Asha Chatterjee had alighted from her abode on the floor above to visit PK in his room. Mishraji tried peeping through the porthole but couldn't manage to find them inside so he thought it to be his solemn responsibility to share this important piece of information with us, especially Shubhom. Shubhom went missing from the office soon afterwards and didn't return till late in the evening.

That evening around eight when we were still waiting for Shubhom to return so that he would clean up the plates and saucepans that we had used for cooking yesterday, we got a call from Inspector Avinash.

"Was Bordoloi in the office today?" the tone of the voice implied he already knew the answer and there was something more serious to it that he wanted to tell us.

"Yes" we obliged "Why? Anything happened"

"Jayanta Bordoloi met with an accident today just outside the town limits. He was in a car and a truck probably a dumper from the coal mines across the brown hills rear-ended him. The impact caused the car to roll over and slide down a 15-metre ditch with a rocky floor. The truck got away and though there were eye-witnesses, nobody managed to see its number plates or identified the driver"

"And Bordoloi, how is he? Is he okay?", Inspector Avinash loved to give news in instalments. That made him feel important.

"Well, the bugger didn't even wear seat belts. Head injury, lots of bleeding, appears to be a lot of fractures as well. He is in a trauma, dropping in and out of consciousness. We have sent him to the surgical ward of the district hospital" he said all of that in an emotionless way in the same way a restaurant waiter recites his menu.

"Will he.... I mean......Is it too serious.... Will he survive?", I had to ask

There was some silence on the other side as if a lot of irritation damming up in him that got manifested as a loud "How the hell should I know?" and then a bit more diplomatic and cinematic way "Well he will survive, I have seen people in worse conditions get through".

Suddenly I remembered something "Inspector Avinash, you know Bordoloi doesn't own a car".

He seemed to be waiting for this "Yes, smarty pants, I am aware of that, the registration plate of the car says that it belongs to your boss. I spoke to your boss too; he had lent it to Bordoloi for the evening."

"Why would he do that?"

"As per your boss, Bordoloi asked for it. He had to attend some function and wanted the car to commute. In your boss's words he must take care of the needs of his colleagues" Avinash replied in a voice drained of any emotion.

"Bad luck for Bordoloi, I had no idea of that".

"Yes, real rotten luck for him but lucky for your boss. This may not be as simple as it seems. This entire setup may be meant for your boss. It was probably another attempt on him, this time by rear-ending his car in the ditch. Someone followed his car but was not aware that Bordoloi was driving it. This time Bordoloi was collateral damage."

I still needed time to compile inspector Avinash's theory. Two failed attempts on our boss, sending two separate individuals to two different hospitals. Yet he remains there hale and hearty making everyone's life connected to him utterly miserable.

"You still there" Avinash derailed my train of thought.

"Yes"

"Try to find out who knew about Bordoloi taking your boss's car. There might be somebody in your office keeping track of your boss's activities even outside the official domain. Call me if you find out anything. As for the car or whatever remains of it, we will be pulling it out as soon as we get a crane from the headquarters. It needs to be checked for any sort of inherent foul play. This has now turned into a high-profile case with the commissioner himself calling up for the case status" he continued his monologue and then as an afterthought he added, "Everything okay with your gang".

Well, I told him that Shubhom hadn't returned till now and he replied with a word that is apt to describe Shubhom but doesn't merit publication in a civilized circle.

Shubhom returned soon after that and I didn't bother asking him where he was. Later when Rajnish cornered him about what he did in the office yesterday when we had gone for lunch, he blurted out everything about the missing files, the photographs in our boss's cupboard, and room 502 in Hotel Shahjahan Regency. He didn't know about Bordoloi's accident or the boss loaning his car to Bordoloi for the evening and also didn't remember why and when he walked out of the office that day. He found himself watching a matinee show of *Pyaasi Jawaani* in Neelam, one of the cinema halls in the marketplace of Baxiganj. He watched the entire show and the subsequent re-run of it in the next show and returned home from there. The rest of the evening he spent listening to sad songs about heartbreak and betrayal until Rajnish removed the batteries of his cassette player and threw them out of the room. This only made him sadder, and he began to sing those songs himself, which was even more unbearable. Rajnish then gave him a Vitamin B complex tablet, telling him that it was a sleeping pill. Shubhom took it and fell asleep within ten minutes, sleeping with the intensity and fervour of Rip Van Winkle.

Rajnish: Third day of the week after the incident

The next day I was sent to visit our *noor-e-daftar* in the district hospital. It was an official trip arranged by our boss who was anxious to find out about Bordoloi's overall condition and specifically concerned about his mental stability. I had orders to do everything possible to get Bordoloi the best possible medical care in the hospital and assure him that PK cares for everyone in the office. PK would have made the trip himself but then the suddenly heightened security restrictions triggered by yesterday's events limited his movement only between the office and his home. I would have to convey that to Bordoloi too if he was in a condition to listen to it.

The hospital was about 15 km downhill from Baxiganj and the road in between cut across the brown hills visible beyond the jungles and winded down to the dusty rolling plains. The district town was built in those plains on the banks of the Subarnarekha by some careless unknown Englishman in a hurry. The road itself was shoddily metalled with its asphalt cover washed away every year during the rains. After the rains, the same road contractor lays another fresh layer of asphalt over it with a precision technology and design that it would last for only one single season of monsoon.

Each time before monsoon the number of potholes in the road almost become equivalent to the population of Baxiganj with an index of per capita one pothole. Accidents are frequent and if something fatal happens the people build a small temple at that spot just to mark the pothole as dangerous. Just a few days back, a schoolteacher returning to Baxiganj on his Rajdoot fell into one of those potholes, lost his balance and got squashed under the wheels of a truck. A general strike of 24 hours was declared to protest against the road conditions. The government machinery gave an ultimatum and the contractors responded by building a new temple overnight to mark the spot and erecting a shining green signboard atop a pole, declaring the area to be accident-prone. The pothole survived unaffected.

This laying and washing of the road had continued iteratively through time with the contractor, engineer and his team remaining a constant feature throughout the road's eventful history. The cumulative amount spent for road maintenance on this road probably reached a level that it would have been entirely possible to build a world-class airport runway connecting these two towns. Monsoons were over and it was road building time again with the smell of asphalt and piles of stone chips making a re-appearance on the roadside. Bordoloi took the same route yesterday before he was supposedly bumped off down one of the cliffs bordering the roads halfway through his journey but this time it wasn't due to the pot-holes.

The driver of my jeep was whistling some tune probably from one of the movies Shubhom keeps on watching. Soon he finished with his whistling or became out of breath and turned towards me and asked "How long had you known Bordoloi?".

"About four months or so", I wasn't in the mood for conversation and tried to reply in an unconcerned voice.

"Well, I have known him for much more than that. Bordoloi lived in our neighbourhood and later I worked as a driver in his department", he went on indifferent to the tone of my reply.

It would have been rude to stop the conversation abruptly there, and, then I felt that the driver wanted to impart some more knowledge about Bordoloi. So, I tried to play along" Was he like the way he is now, even when you knew him?".

The driver didn't bother about my question. He had by then planned his narrative and set about narrating that in his style "Bordoloi belonged to a place called Namrup in Assam where his father was a manager in a fertilizer company. He became a part of Pioneer after his graduation through a recruitment drive aimed at the employment of local youths. After that, Bordoloi was absorbed in the Tinsukia office of PMO in the capacity of a junior technical assistant in the Geology Section."

He stopped as if to find out if I was still interested in Bordoloi's life history. I egged him on with a question I was interested in "Did he do any work there?"

"Well, he did." The driver continued his storytelling while dribbling his jeep through crater-sized potholes "The work assigned to him was surveying and erecting pillars in areas where an oil well was proposed to be drilled. Additionally, he also acted as an agent for the company to acquire the land from the landowner by deciding on a compensatory price. Surprisingly, Bordoloi excelled in both these jobs without anybody helping or bothering him. They even gave him an award for his work."

"So, if he was so good in his work, why did he even get transferred to Baxiganj?"

The driver seemed to be expecting this question "His luck ran out. Everything was in such a cloud nine mode for Bordoloi. But then, suddenly after two years, a service firm selling GPS services conducted a pilot survey in a small part of the PMO's upper Assam acreages. The results of the survey showed that some pillars erected by Bordoloi were off from the actual location by about 500 metres or even more."

"Well, that is really bad", I didn't know what to say about that

"There were some departmental investigations. They revealed more such cases in which Bordoloi planted the pillars in the wrong places. Most of these pillars were in lands of owners from where he got a hefty kickback amount for its acquisition.". The driver was now enjoying his rendition of the rise and fall of Bordoloi.

"What?" This was really beyond expectations for me.

The driver was waiting for such a response. He moved to a higher gear with his account, his eyes twinkling with some newly acquired energy, "These locations when drilled either turned out to be dry wells or performed below expectation. The Geology Section didn't want to investigate this issue any further fearing backlash from the headquarters. They cancelled all the remaining locations and transferred Bordoloi overnight to Baxiganj where all lands were forest lands and hence there was no scope of getting any sort of kickbacks. Bordoloi was posted in this office and assigned several non-technical jobs which mainly involved handling of files and passing on and receiving messages to well sites and field bases."

So that was Bordoloi on an entirely new level. PK must have been aware of all this and yet there seemed to be a comfortable symbiosis between both of them in office and outside.

The driver hadn't yet finished with his story "I had accompanied Bordoloi a couple of times during his trips to plant pillars. But I never knew what he was doing. Yet they transferred me with him to Baxiganj."

Well, that was then the entire purpose of the story, a mix of vengeance against Bordoloi for dragging him to Baxiganj and the need to clear his name from the mess that Bordoloi carried with him. And then the story also made Baxiganj a sort of dumping ground for tainted people- a strange choice of place to start our careers. I had a hunch that there was something more to read into it, but then that can wait.

In the hospital, I couldn't locate Bordoloi even after making two rounds in the surgical ward. If it hadn't been for the attendant I would have missed him altogether. Ultimately, I found him hidden under multiple layers of bandages and plasters tucked up in a corner bed and half asleep probably under the effect of sedatives. Only part of his face and one of his swollen eyes were visible with the rest of it covered under bandages making him look sinister like somebody from a horror movie. A tube carried some pale liquid from a hanging bottle through his nose while another tube was attached to his crotch area to empty his bladder. As per the attendant, Bordoloi had a broken jaw, his right arm was fractured at multiple places, and several ribs were broken along with a dislocated hip joint. The doctors still couldn't ascertain if there was any head injury and if his mental facilities were working properly and needed to observe him further for a proper diagnosis. He will need more than a month to get patched up properly and climb out of that bed and a further indefinite time to walk normally again without any support.

No one from his family was there beside him so I had to complete all the required formalities, get his medicines from the pharmacy, and arrange for an attendant who would be personally attending to him round the clock. When I returned to his bed after completing all of these and sat near him, Bordoloi was awake and groaning. His only visible eye showed a sign of recognition and tried to say something to me, nothing of which was coherent or distinct. I tried to move myself as close as possible to Bordoloi's face to gather what he was muttering. At first, it didn't make sense, he appeared to be repeatedly chanting something like "Om" but then when I listened to it more carefully, I got what he was saying, "Shubhom" over and over. All my senses froze momentarily. I needed more information on how was Shubhom a part of all this. Bordoloi was just fuelling up my worst thoughts. Bordoloi by the time had dozed off again into semi-consciousness. I tried to shake him awake but then the ward doctor stepped in at the moment and asked me to leave him alone.

The return journey was an unusually quiet one with both the driver and me choosing to stay silent throughout the journey. The sun was setting behind us above the district town and illuminated everything with a golden tinge as we climbed up the winding road to Baxiganj. A flock of birds flew over the river into the darkness of the jungle beyond it in a shape-shifting formation. I tried to ruminate on whatever Shubhom told us yesterday about PK's cupboard and its contents and work on probable scenarios of what may have happened. According to Shubhom, there was an empty file cover with all its contents missing. That implied somebody might have taken it out. Now since our boss had the primary access to this data, it could be assumed that he was the one who brought it out into sunshine. Shubhom saw him enter Raman's room in his hotel and PK knew Raman from his induction days. That raises a high possibility that both were collaborating on the smuggling of the data from Pioneer to PetroIndia. PK probably had handed over our data to Raman. But then if Raman had got the data, there was no reason for him to shoot at our boss. Maybe the deal between them, for some reason went sour and Raman wanted to remove all traces that would implicate him in this data smuggling. And now that he knew who was trying to get him killed, PK might be arm-twisting Raman to get something more substantial out of the deal.

There might be another possibility where there might be other contenders who also wanted to get those maps like Raman. It could be possible that one of these contenders wanted to eliminate PK. But that seemed a bit unlikely since no other companies had shown their interest in this area. However, two bullets were fired at PK followed by another attempt to finish him off on this road. From those events, it did seem that somebody wanted PK out of their way. The only person in the entire gamut of the investigation, who would have derived the maximum quantum of benefit from a dead PK would be Raman, the person surprisingly equipped with a nuclear missile-proof alibi. That brings into the equation someone who would operate behind the shadows of Raman fulfilling his vendetta to get rid of PK. Someone, I didn't want to think of. However, each time I tried to mentally re-create the scene the same face floated and formed before me. Something appeared to be terribly wrong in the sequence of events. Yet I just couldn't figure that out. My train of thought hit a dead end and jumbled up beyond that.

The map could have been the cornerstone of this entire conundrum but it was missing. However, the missing map must have had a copy of it in the Geophysical Services Department or GSD where it was originally recorded. I decided to call up my batchmate Ravi posted in the GSD asking him to provide the date and group that had logged this info.

That evening, I accosted Shubhom once more asking him again where he was after disappearing from the office yesterday. He decided to remain a crackpot and continued his story about *Pyaasi Jawaani* in Neelam. This time he even added that the heroine of the movie looked like Asha Chatterjee and that's why he saw the movie twice. He was now seeing her everywhere. But then the question remained why would Bordoloi take Shubhom's name and whether there was any connection between him and Bordoloi's accident. While returning from the hospital, the driver had stopped the jeep at the place where Bordoloi's car or rather PKs car had gone off the road into the cliff. It was twilight, and from the edge of the cliff, the bottom appeared to be almost 15 metres deep shrouded in a thick cover of semi-darkness. I tried to think of ways in which a screwball like Shubhom could get a 1.2-ton vehicle driven by a 35-year-old shrewd man to dive down a 50-foot cliff into that darkness but couldn't fancy anything practical. Inspector Avinash's theory of somebody pushing off Bordoloi assuming him to be our boss was far sounder and more believable.

Ravi's call came the next day when we were in the office. He wanted to meet us in person in exactly one hour, in the cafeteria and added that it was a serious issue. Ravi was always serious about everything in his job profile. Before joining Pioneer, he had nursed ambitions to join the army but then gave up after two failed attempts in SSB. From then onwards he cultivated and practised all those criteria needed to be a cadet in the army from maintaining a buzz-cut hairstyle, black shiny shoes, and perfectly ironed clothes to considering all his jobs as some sort of operations. I found him in the cafeteria looking at his watch just to make me aware that I was late for the appointment even though he had attributed it with words like sharp. I decided to directly come to my question rather than being endured to a full lecture on punctuality along with specific case studies about the devastating effects of not being on time- "Did you get the info we talked about yesterday?"

Ravi brought out a piece of paper from his pocket and then began to read from it "At 2000, yesterday got your call requesting info on the maps. At 0930 today started searching all the archival tapes stored in GSD for the Tandwa maps, results were negative. At 1030 checked all the registers to find out which geophysical party recorded this data. However, the results were again negative, none of the campaigns since the inception of GSD showed any party recording seismic data in Tandwa. At 1130 fixed up an appointment with the co-ordinator of all data acquisition parties. He checked his registers and informed me that there was no record of such a map."

"So, what next?" I asked.

Ravi continued reading from his paper "So finally at 1200 hours I decided to call my boss, the chief of all geophysical acquisition parties to find out about your Tandwa maps. He categorically told me to stand down and stop asking questions where I wasn't concerned, for things that are way above my pay grade"

That seemed to be the end of Ravi's efforts, so I just thought of safely exiting the scene "Thanks for all your efforts, see you around"

Ravi wasn't still finished. He scribbled something on the paper, folded it neatly and put it in his pocket and then asked "Well, I am not done? I need to know why I am putting myself in the line of fire for this map of yours?"

This wasn't something I wanted to discuss with him at this time. I tried the safest way out. "Ravi, I need to check the name of the place again, maybe there was a mistake. I will get back to you after that. But anyway thanks."

Ravi was clenching and unclenching his fists, trying to fix his burn-everything gaze on something beyond me "What do you mean you need to check again? I spent the entire morning looking for your map. You could be court-martialled if you were in the army. Anyway, I am out of this." He marched out of the cafeteria like a jilted lover making enough noise to make sure that everyone there noticed him retreating.

Ramanujam:

About 2 weeks after the incident

The next few days in the office were peaceful with our boss consciously avoiding us as if he was afraid or embarrassed about something. There were no morning meetings anymore and our boss began to spend less and less time in the office staying mostly at his home. Suddenly all his bravura vanished, and he was paranoid that somebody might be waiting to kill him if he ventured out too much. There was always a retinue of security behind him wherever he moved, even inside the office. One day, the executive assistant to the GM informed us that our boss had moved a file for his immediate transfer back to Delhi and most probably it would be agreed upon. They were looking for people who would replace him, but no name has been formalized as of yet.

His wife showed no signs of any recovery and remained in the ICU of the Baxiganj hospital. Bordoloi on the other hand had undergone several surgeries in the district hospital and needed to be shifted to a bigger and better hospital for further treatment. He still couldn't speak clearly or move his limbs. Inspector Avinash informed that they got the boss's car out of the ditch but couldn't test it for any tampering. It was completely damaged, and Bordoloi was lucky to be alive in whatever state he was. Rajnish got himself busy in the office searching around and checking old files, noting bits of info from them in his notebook and discussing them with Inspector Avinash in long evening sessions. Somehow, he had convinced Inspector Avinash that he was the only person outside the police force who could help him and his help was absolutely necessary to crack this case. He even took my car to visit Bordoloi in his hospital a couple of times with just an explanation or an excuse that Bordoloi needed help and he needed information.

The day we got the news of PK's impending transfer, our home-grown nincompoop, Shubhom mustered some more courage, dressed up in a red shirt, redder than Lenin, Mao and Che Guvera put together and a yellow polka-dotted scarf, went upstairs, and continued staring at Asha Chatterjee. It was difficult to determine whether he wanted to serenade her or find out if she acted in *Pyaasi Jawaani*. However, it didn't help him and after a couple of attempts, she changed positions—this time with her back facing him.

Shubhom didn't give up hope; he left a long letter in her diary and a deodorant on her table. Asha Chatterjee returned Shubhom the letter without even opening it but kept the deodorant with her. This, fortunately for us, marked the end of Shubhom's *Staring Satyagraha* and he returned to his place on the floor below, dejected and morose. Usually, this type of situation often leads to Shubhom either singing or playing those sad songs that dunk you into the pits of depression and self-pity leaving you groggy and emotionally drained. To prevent this from happening again Rajnish planned to take Shubhom to Ramlal's Café in one of the by-lanes of the main market, where at least we would be spared from the side effects of his broken heart. At the cafeteria, Usha Uthhup was already singing from the insides of a sound system, denying Shubhom any chance to sing his songs. To compensate for that, he stuffed his mouth with most of the food we ordered as if that was his way of taking revenge on PK for snatching Asha Chatterjee from him.

Halfway through our meal, Inspector Avinash made an appearance, this time without his uniform. He straight away walked to our table, pulled a chair and ordered a cup of coffee as if he knew we would be there at that time. I didn't want to be rude asking uncomfortable questions but then everything in the situation suggested that it was probably a set-up planned by Rajnish. We ate our food in silence when predictably Rajnish posed his first question "What do you think happened to the maps?"

"It had been handed over to Raman and all traces of it obliterated." I guessed

"How did you assume that?", this time it was Inspector Avinash, not even looking at us, nonchalantly finishing his coffee. So, this was morphing into a brainstorming session.

"If our boss gave the map to Raman, why would he shoot our boss or have him shot at and why is Bordoloi in the hospital today?", Rajnish added to the question.

I couldn't answer the question, Shubhom did. "Somebody may not have liked this transfer of documents, so he tried to have our boss killed, or maybe Raman did not want to take any risks, so he wanted to remove all traces and all evidences."

"Okay, that's what most of us will be thinking, let us try this from another angle- *ek mutabaadil nazariya*. Have you seen the map?"

There was no reply. None among us had ever seen the map or understood what Rajnish's Urdu meant or if such a word existed.

"What if the map didn't exist?" Rajnish asked again. This time the inspector kept aside his coffee and looked at us as if he waiting for us to give our opinions before revealing his judgement.

Anyway, according to me it was a crazy question. "Everybody in the office asserted the existence of the maps. It was the reason that our boss almost got killed twice and two people went to the hospital. Even the file covers of the map existed, indicating the maps were there and had been stolen. If those maps got stolen, then the maps should have existed." I ended up almost breathless trying to build a logic.

"Yet, the GSD says that the data never got recorded in the first place. If the data isn't recorded, how can the maps ever be made." Rajnish was taking this discussion towards a direction that I still couldn't figure out.

"So, what do you want to imply?" I was still disoriented.

"That the maps never existed in the first place. It was some kind of Urban Legend floated by the higher en-echelons of this company. Do you know, of all the places why they selected Baxiganj as the Regional Headquarters of this company? This is the current chief minister's hometown. Likewise, this chief minister wants to show the development and employment of this area by keeping PMO here. But, by then, Pioneer had already drilled seven dry wells. It was at this juncture someone at the highest management had manufactured and launched this urban legend about the maps of Tandwa. PK and the GM just played along, strengthening this legend."

Inspector Avinash nodded in assertion. All this appeared to be discussed earlier. We were just a sounding board to check out the ideas.

"Okay, agreed. But then why was Raman interested in this block?"

"No, he wasn't. Raman was your boss's batchmate and friend. He just played his part in consolidating this misconception, maybe for some favour that he would cash in later?" It was the inspector now "We have already got permission to monitor and record their calls. There was one call recorded at the exchange that established they knew each other well enough and there was some kind of plan between them. Once we get some more evidence, we will bring Raman in."

"Okay even if it is so, what about us?", Shubhom was worried now.

"Us? Do you remember the guy who came for recruitment from PMO? He specifically told us that we were the only ones who had in them what the company needed.

"Yes,", Shubhom recalled., "He specifically said that we were the only ones among the entire lot who had it in them what the company needs."

"Yes," Rajnish said. "Precisely, *bilkul durust*, we were fools, and that was what PMO needed at that point in time. People who would blindly follow orders. We were just digging a ditch and filling it again and repeating the same thing over and over. Jobs that meant nothing to the company, yet, were necessary to show that the company was working. PK knew that and used us. PK was aware of all our weaknesses, including those of Bordoloi and Asha Chatterjee and then exploited them. But there was one thing he miscalculated. Our curiosity. He never expected Shubhom to break his safe and find out that the maps were missing."

Suddenly, the food before me didn't seem so tasty at all and the girls around us dissolved in the greyish background of the café. I was no stranger to being taken advantage of, but it drained away any self-esteem I had. All the maps that I had made for two complete months turned up to be bogus. The fieldwork in the jungles was just a sham. The conference which Rajnish attended with all its lectures was just an elaborate façade to cover up a lie. The files that never came to a conclusion and just went around like ping-pong balls were all part of this.

"So, why was our boss shot at?". I still hoped that Rajnish's entire theory was wrong.

"Oh, that's another part of the story. Your boss was not shot at. The bullets were fired for his wife, and they did their job."

"Why would anyone want to kill the boss's wife?"

"Not anyone, the boss wanted to kill his wife. Raman just helped him through." Rajnish took over from the inspector.

"Well, Raman seems to have a very extended guest appearance in this case," I tried to give some input to the discussion.

"Yes, that's how this case appears to be strategized.", Avinash picked up his coffee mug, drank whatever residue was left inside and continued, "Everything was planned in a way that portrays Raman as the most visible showpiece in every aspect of the case. Yet he had solid pitch perfect alibis- something that led us to expend more and more effort in finding holes in them to frame him. That led to the case getting diverted on an entirely separate track to an entirely different station."

"And then", Shubhom appeared to have recovered from his morose Devdas mode

"Then you invaded PK's cupboard, it turned out to be a catalyst of sorts. Skeletons stumbled out, skeletons vanished, and for the first time, another portal opened up showing the beautiful face of your Lady Chatterjee. That led us to think beyond Raman"

"And you were right about it, the girl in Pyaasi Jawaani was indeed Asha Chatterjee. She did moonlight as an actress in a few B-grade movies. Now that brings in a new angle to our case and you might also have a change in perspective about her."

That was a once-in-a-leap-year moment when two people praised Shubhom consecutively and that too for his fallacy. Shubhom, however, didn't bother to show any reaction to anything that was being said.

"It was only during the investigations following Bordoloi's accident that we got to know that Raman is just a non-entity, a decoy used to side-track this investigation."

"Just like Jewel Thief" Shubhom was in an elated state of mind and wanted to add something to Inspector Avinash's analysis.

"What?", Inspector Avinash wasn't familiar with Shubhom's expertise in Bollywood.

"North by Northwest, Cary Grant", Shubhom shifted to Hollywood. That too was out of range for Inspector Avinash

"I am only familiar with Clint Eastwood, Dirty Harry. Anyway, where was I, okay, PK wanted to get out of the relationship, remove the leash that his father-in-law had put around him and get rid of his wife, his mother-in-law, and her dog who was making life hell for him as he did for you. Also, he had more than a soft corner for Asha Chatterjee and was having an affair with her, which he needed to hide from everyone and wanted all of his family out of the way. First, he built up the situation around the Tandwa maps so that the entire focus was on him as a victim. Then he brought Raman from Delhi and installed him in Hotel Shahjahan Regency as a face for everything he did in the background. Both of them arranged for an assassin and an eyewitness who would mislead the police."

Shubhom was now staring at Avinash in the same way he did at Asha Chatterjee. Avinash ignored him and went on, "Your boss is five feet eleven and sat in the front of the Lambretta. His wife is five feet four and sits behind him. So, it was an impossible angle to shoot at her from the building. The only way to get her was if the vehicle stopped and PK got off from the scooter."

"How can you be so sure of that", I still wasn't convinced

This time again it was Inspector Avinash, "We had forensics done. Mostly you can say that we had got footprints of PK and none of his wife in the zone of the incident. This led to the probability that his wife didn't alight from the scooter but PK did."

“There’s no proof, he could have got down from the scooter even after the bullet hit his wife and his footprints would still be there.”, I interrupted Avinash, cutting him midway through his explanation.

For a moment it appeared that the inspector’s jaw tightened a bit and his eyebrows furrowed. He picked up a butter knife from the table and studied it for a moment until his features relaxed and he began again.

“Okay, let’s start over, PK was riding a Lambretta with a kerb weight of about 135 kgs going at a speed of around 50 km per hour with his wife in the pillion. Do you concur?”

I looked at the knife in his hand and nodded meekly.

“Good, now let’s say PK applied brakes the moment he realized the bullet hit his wife. What do you expect would have happened?” He pointed the question at me.

I wasn’t mentally prepared to react to that question at that moment.”

“Well, we recreated the scene with these exact parameters. The scooter stopped at least 5 metres over-shooting the point of impact after braking.”

Inspector Avinash was now on a roll, and I guessed what was about to come.

"And surprise, the only footprints that we got were of PK and exactly at the point of impact. Well, for your kind information, he wears a size 8 shoe on his left foot and a size 9 on his right with his right foot impression more prominent than his left. And to add to it, forensics got some skid marks on the spot in the road that matched the scooter's tyre, implying that brakes were applied much earlier than what your boss wanted us to believe. And lastly, that was also the spot, where the police got the scooter. You got it wise-ass"

The butter knife was still in his hand with its business end pointed straight at me. I had to nod.

Avinash was waiting for the nod, "Right, so PK stopped his Lambretta at the designated point, put it on the side stand, got down, moved away from it and that was his signal for the shooter to do his job. And, that was how it happened. Again, I can't divulge everything before you at this moment but broadly this was what possibly happened. Any more questions?".

"He could have asked for a divorce instead of investing in such trouble," Shubhom asked.

"I don't know, maybe he couldn't afford the alimony or maybe his wife wasn't willing to give one or maybe his father-in-law would have toppled his career in case of divorce. This was a more convenient option for him that suited all his purposes."

"And, what about Bordoloi.?"

"Yes", it was Rajnish this time. "Bordoloi had no idea of the maps but he knew about Asha Chatterjee's photographs in PK's safe and PK's bluff to Asha Chatterjee about arranging her posting in the Establishment. That day when PK suspected that somebody had opened his safe and we had to cover for Shubhom, do you remember the extra-long meeting between boss and Bordoloi and then another one between Asha Chatterjee and PK."

"Yes. We do."

"In the first one, Bordoloi tried some sort of blackmail on PK This probably led to the second meeting between Lady Chatterjee and our boss."

I was going to ask something but he precluded the scenario, "The blackmail part was confirmed by Bordoloi himself when I met him later. Bordoloi will now be shifted to a safe medical facility and after recovery, there are chances of him turning witness."

Rajnish then pointed at Shubhom across the table "Well, your Asha Chatterjee is now a bonafide suspect in an attempt to murder charge. Think about that".

"So am I", Shubhom interrupted in an almost sub-audible tone.

"Yes, super-chef, you are a suspect but we can come to it later. First, let's hear a bit more about your sweetheart. Baxiganj police did a bit of background check on her and came out with something unexpected". Avinash brought out a comb from his pocket and began to comb his already combed and gelled hair. "Asha Chatterjee was an orphan and lived with her relatives who didn't want her hanging around them for long. After completing her graduation, she worked in a local theatre company where she came across her erst-while boyfriend who promised to be her support and meet all her needs. This boyfriend of hers found our lady had ambitions way beyond her means and taking advantage of that lured her to the world of seedy cinemas and dumped her there. There she got entrapped and helpless without an escape route and had to act in a few B-grade movies just for sustenance. She eventually found her way out through a producer who also happened to be the son-in-law of a sitting MLA and got herself a job in PMO. And then your boss brought her to your office and the rest you know."

We nodded in silence- we did know what happened after that in detail.

"Well, what you don't know is that his boyfriend was a school teacher and after dumping her got married and settled in the district town from where he used to commute daily to Baxiganj'"

"So?", Shubhom was getting impatient".

"A few days back, that boyfriend was crushed to paste beneath a truck on the road to Baxiganj.' The truck coincidentally happened to be from the same mine from which a dumper rear-ended Bordoloi."

Shubhom let out an almost inaudible gasp. Avinash eyed him once and continued with his tale "And like Bordoloi's incident, the driver disappeared. never to be found again." Here Avinash paused a bit, made sure that his collar was properly folded and then placed his muffler over it so that it looked like a scarf. Finally, he said "Well, the next part of what might have happened will be deliberated by your friend,"

Rajnish took over. "Once Asha Chatterjee got to know that Bordoloi had got a whiff of their affair and was attempting blackmail, things were no longer smooth for her. A lot of things, including her new-found career, were at stake. She didn't want to climb down the ladder again and get back into her dark days. So, this time both of them devised a strategy to eliminate Bordoloi."

Rajnish stopped for breath, mistook my glass to be his and drank a gulp of water from it'

"As a part of their plan our boss gave his car to Bordoloi, sent him on an errand to the district town and then had him bumped into a cliff with a truck. The truck was arranged on an emergency basis by our MLA's son-in-law. It belonged to one of his fleets that worked in the coal mines in which he has a substantial share. We all assumed it to be another attempt on PK by someone who was after the maps."

"And then PK sent you to find out about him in the hospital", I tried to add to Rajnish's analysis.

"Yes, the job didn't end up as per expectations. Asha Chatterjee got nervous when she found that Bordoloi was alive. Both of them didn't want any loose ends. So, at her behest, PK sent me to the hospital to specifically find out if Bordoloi was mentally stable meaning if there were chances that he would blurt out everything he was trying to blackmail PK with. Asha Chatterjee was probably pressuring PK to finish off Bordoloi in the hospital itself, but then PK had already chickened out and started to act spooked to avoid us and even Asha Chatterjee. He had by then applied for transfer out of Baxiganj." Rajnish stopped as if he remembered something important "That day in the hospital when Bordoloi repeated Shubhom's name, I thought he was trying to implicate Shubhom in his accident but then later, I realized that he was trying to save him. Bordoloi somehow suspected that PK had orchestrated his accident. He also guessed that Shubhom had opened PK's safe, saw Asha Chatterjee's photos and thus ran the risk of getting eliminated like him. So, he wanted to warn us that Shubhom may be the next victim of PK or from a broader perspective even Asha Chatterjee"

“So why...”, I wanted to ask why nothing happened to Shubhom but realized what I would be saying and stayed silent.

Rajnish guessed my predicament and went on “There may be two things or a mixture of them. One she realized that there was nothing to fear or Shubhom would not be causing any harm to her or secondly Shubhom was the only person who for whatever reasons loved her without thinking of taking advantage of her.”

Rajnish stopped and turned towards Shubhom. Shubhom’s facial expression was incomprehensible in the darkness of the restaurant. The revolving multi-coloured disco lights played on his face but nothing except his still eyes and clenched lips were visible. He probably plastered his salesman-type smile over his face that was supposed to mask any change of feelings that he was experiencing.

An uneasy bout of silence engulfed our table with no one attempting to explain or question anything. All of us chose to listen to Usha Uthup as if it had just dawned upon us, what a legendary singer she is. Inspector Avinash probably felt uncomfortable living within the fleeting shroud of silence and chose to break it by clearing his throat. He pulled out his packet of Charminar, tapped a cigarette and lit one, blew his rings, waited for them to disappear, and said,

"That, gentlemen, was the gist of whatever may have happened", Inspector Avinash finished his coffee and seemed to be preparing to leave the table. "However, this is the point where you get off the case. I needed your help and thanks to you we have advanced a fair bit on this case. We have established a motive and are zeroing in on the accused and with some luck may be able to close the case soon. However, I doubt whether PK will be giving you any reward for this. Consider this coffee to be a treat for you from me. Please continue and order whatever you like. I will be taking your leave. Will be meeting you again."

Inspector Avinash left the cafeteria without paying, settling the bill with just a nod towards the manager of the cafeteria.

"What now?", I asked Rajnish, worried about our future and he seemed to be the only one to have some answers about that. Rajnish didn't appear to be too much troubled with our future prospects and was more concerned at that time getting our tabletop reloaded with another layer of snacks. This was very much typical of him, showing off his immense coolness even in the heat of things.

Once he had loaded his deck with food sufficient to feed an entire town of Mogadishu, he started with an egg roll, and after ensuring half of it was in his mouth replied "Don't know,", and after finishing it added. "As for us at present, the GM's executive assistant informed me that all of us will be transferred. Ramanujam is going to Bombay, me to Delhi, and Shubhom to Bangalore, and we were advised to keep our mouth shut.". Usha Utthup had stopped singing and was replaced by Asha Bhonsle belting out "O *Haseena Zulfowali*."

Shubhom had stopped eating since he had heard of Bordoloi trying to save him and was engrossed somewhere in his 'Main aur Meri Tanhai' corner of his universe. "Shubhom, who gave you the plan to steal those maps from PK" Rajnish pointed his question towards him.

"Bunty, we would have given it back," he replied.

"And. Who helped you do it?"

"Bunty," he replied again.

"Where is he now?"

"Well, he isn't here; he keeps busy with his work", Shubhom now started picking French fries from the plate and nibbling them nervously.

"When did you last see him.?"

"Just before coming here."

"And I bet you were making some plans about PK or your Senorita,"

"Yes, we did but why are we having this conversation?"

For the first time, I agreed with Shubhom. I couldn't figure out anything about the exchange.

Again, there was a silence as if Rajnish was getting ready to tell something or thinking of a way to tell that or maybe thinking if at all he should tell that. I could feel my breathing become faster and a churning feeling in my stomach in anticipation of something that had gone wrong. Meanwhile, Asha Bhonsle had finished all three stanzas of O *Haseena* and moved on to *Jawani Jaaneman*, transcending from Helen to Parveen Babi. Oblivious to all these, Shubhom was devouring the French fries one after another as if he too was under stress and preparing for something extraordinary.

It appeared to be almost the end of a geological epoch when Rajnish finally spoke up,

"Shubhom, we had been friends since college but now as you know will be parting our ways soon. Hence, it is necessary to tell you. Please listen to me carefully. There is no one called Bunty among us. Bunty is a part of you that you had created. A smarter version of you, a mixture of all your heroes that you invoke when things get tough. Though you can communicate, he doesn't exist. Everything was done by you, you. You planned the entire cracking off PK's cupboard, you searched for the maps without the help of anyone, and it was because of you that PK got exposed. You don't need Bunty for doing things you can do."

Shubhom remained unmoved and unfazed. The only thing that appeared to mirror his condition were his eyeballs which remained fixed on the plate before him as if he was going to bore a hole through them with his eyes. I just couldn't fathom his condition -his face was deliberately opaque as if trying to shield his vulnerability from us. There were some signs of disbelief in his eyes that appeared to mutate into anger but then were erased of all expressions.

As far as I got to know Rajnish, he wasn't a sensitive person but still, he tried his best to soothe Shubhom down, "It might take time but eventually you need to forget him, let Bunty go. We are your friends, real ones in flesh and blood. You don't need imaginary entities."

Suddenly Shubhom got up and walked out of the restaurant, his shoulders hunched like a defeated and lonely man making his way in life, trying to find his elusive identity. We weren't even sure if the individual who walked out was Shubhom or Bunty. Rajnish's words had no impact on him.

This was really beyond my wildest expectations. I needed a moment to compile the un-realness of everything that just unravelled before me and then ran out to bring Shubhom back. However, by then the evening crowd had engulfed him or he had chosen to hide in the crowd so that we wouldn't find him. I knew Shubhom to be somewhat weird, a bit different from us, forgetting things and living in the past but never thought it to be a result of two separate personalities. When the smarter version takes over Shubhom gets those fits of forgetfulness.

When I returned to our table, Rajnish was sitting there with a blank face.

"You knew all along about Bunty, didn't you?"

"No, I just tried to guess his patterns of forgetfulness and his mumblings to himself. But believe me, I just wanted him to live his own life." Rajnish was trying to convince me or rather justify himself.

"Why did he choose the name Bunty?"

"I can just hazard a guess. Well, once he told me that the first movie that he remembered to have watched was '*Love Story*'. I found out that Bunty was the name of the hero in the movie."

There was still one bit of puzzle that didn't seem to fit in. At least I couldn't figure it out. Since Rajnish didn't clear it out, I had to specify, "What happened that night after the party? Where did Shubhom go when he walked out of the restaurant?"

Rajnish seemed to be waiting to answer this question for a long time. He fished around the plate for some bits of French fries that Shubhom might have left, found some and then began "That evening I saw Shubhom walking out of the restaurant after the girl but couldn't figure out where he had gone. Later when we were relating the events of the day to Inspector Avinash, I deliberately left this part out since I wanted to find it out myself and didn't want to get into trouble at that moment. What I gathered from a few shopkeepers who still had their shops open was that Shubhom did go towards PK's house and landed at the back of it. There he probably hurled some stones and shouted some abuses which PK's mother-in-law heard and construed as signals of doom. Shubhom might have left when she reached the roof with her torch and from there, he trudged back home content at the fact that he had at least avenged PK to some extent."

Our orders for transfer came within a week. At the station, Inspector Avinash came to see us away. Nepal Police had caught a suspect in Biratnagar and a team from Baxiganj was on their way to get him. PK has been sent away on leave with orders to stay within the limits of Baxiganj.

Apart from Inspector Avinash, Mishraji came to the station to see off Shubhom with a gift in his hand. The gift, it turned out was from Asha Chatterjee with Mishraji acting only as her delivery guy for her. Despite everything that happened, Shubhom's eyes lit up like the headlights of a Chetak scooter as soon as he saw the gift and learnt about the sender. He hurriedly tore open the packing to reveal its contents- a bottle of deodorant, which was different from the one that Shubhom had gifted her. He kept it aside and frantically kept on searching for something more- but there was nothing: no messages, no address, no promises, nothing more.

Epilogue:

Ramanujam: 12 years later

Twelve years had passed since that evening when Shubhom had walked out of the restaurant. In these twelve years, I had completed my Ph.D., left my job at Pioneer, and joined a research institute in Mumbai. Also, in these twelve years, I lost touch with many people who had once been my support system, and I didn't even miss them. My father had retired as a dean from his university and had now settled in Hyderabad as a faculty in a private university. He tries to maintain some form of contact and I am happy with that. Over the years, I understood why people felt that I was snobbish, and so I tried to mellow down and respect others. I tried to catch up with Aditi, the girl I had ditched, and apologize to her, but she had moved on in her life and didn't even return my calls. I tried to trim down my expectations and make them more realistic. Many new things happened to me that complicated my life, making me more complex, more practical, and less idealistic, and shaping a new locus for me. Yet it was the memories of Baxiganj that remained permanently etched in my mind. I longed to return to Baxiganj many times, just to touch base, to trigger an invisible and imaginary reset button that would take me back to the innocent and uncomplicated me that I knew I once was and would never become again. Yet, each time I indulge in these thoughts, something creeps up and drives these useless nostalgic feelings back to the ante-room of my brain. The only connection I still had with Baxiganj was Rajnish. He was still in Pioneer's Delhi office, in the same place where PK was before being posted to Baxiganj. Now, Rajnish's work involves making animated presentations about corporate policies. I even tried to get in touch with Shubhom, just to find out how he was dealing with life, but he chose to remain hidden and incommunicado, just like that evening in Baxiganj.

It was at a conference in Delhi that I had run into Rajnish again. We decided to catch up, and he invited me to his home where we were served chicken and puri for dinner by Sunny. I asked him about Shubhom and he told me that he was still in Bangalore. He had gotten married but had compatibility issues with his wife, so he eventually got a divorce. He was now leading life as a bachelor, desperately seeking someone like Asha Oberoi again. He had even gone into depression and had to take a year off from his job. Though he had joined back now, he had lost his promotion and was trying to cope with life.

His views about Communism had also changed. He had come to the conclusion that maybe communism could be the only way of handling a new nation or culture, but once it had advanced or grown, it was best to discontinue it as a rule, otherwise, a nation might end up underdeveloped, stifled, and extremely corrupt. His Durgapur, however, had developed into an exemplary, beautiful, planned city, and a major industrial and educational hub with many of its second-generation citizens– besides Shubhom–established far and wide as professionals in various fields.

PK had retired without any further promotions and was also presently settled in Delhi. His wife had died in the Baxiganj hospital after suffering for almost a month but was never conscious enough to reveal what had exactly happened that night. PK was arrested and charged with IPC sections 302 and 307, but his lawyer argued in court that all the evidence presented against him was circumstantial and inadequate to be admissible as proof and the judge had agreed to that. The actual shooter who shot PK's wife, or the driver who rear-ended Bordoloi were never found. In the end, the judge dismissed the case and PK was acquitted, becoming a free man in every sense of the word. Inspector Avinash was still in contact with Rajnish. He had been the lead investigating officer of the case throughout its course, and even though the verdict of the case came to a dead end, he had risen in the ranks and was presently a DSP. All of Bordoloi's medical bills were paid by the police. He was presented as a witness against PK in court, but when questioned, he turned hostile, feigning complete memory loss due to the accident. He, too, never received any other promotions during his career, became an alcoholic, and ultimately was forced to accept voluntary retirement. He still lives in Baxiganj, stays alone in his house, and walks with a limp–the only thing he got for serving PK. There was no case against Raman and all the efforts of police to track him down failed. People say that he fled to Dubai and settled there, running his businesses from the Middle - East. Asha Chatterjee had no lingering feelings for anyone and had gotten married to an executive of PMO in the same year that we had left and PK got arrested. There was no evidence against her and she wasn't even arrested. When questioned, she denied any connection to the case and threatened with harassment charges if she was questioned any further. She was now the head of Human Resources at Baxiganj Pioneer Oil. There was no news about the whereabouts of Mishraji.

A few months after the case was closed; local newspapers reported an accident in a colliery near Baxiganj where a dumper dumped a carriage full of coal on a person called Deepak Kapoor who also happened to be the son-in-law of a sitting MLA. That piece of news somehow reached PK and triggered in him a belief that it was now his turn to die and their people were lurking around just waiting to kill him. This made him paranoid, and he started to stay indoors with all his doors and windows shut. All people who were employed as house-helps in his apartment were removed from their service. PK isolated himself completely forbidding anyone from visiting his home. Gradually, he began to have panic attacks, shouted at invisible people and started to suspect everyone including his close friends and relatives of trying to murder him. Last heard, he is still alive but had turned into a complete lunatic.

Pioneer Minerals & Oil Incorporates in Baxiganj continued to run, fuelled by the legend of the maps of Tandwa–an *afsana* in Rajnish's Urdu. Many young people had joined there after us and mapped and modelled the area, many conferences had been arranged, inviting out-of-the-box ideas, yet, the area remained just on the verge of success. This was until someone from another division of Pioneer discovered commercial quantities of Coal Bed Methane outside the mapped area, based on an experimental study. This led to a change in the entire exploration plan with several new wells being drilled in the shallow coal seams outside Baxiganj. New power plants and fertilizer industries were set up there that were fuelled by the gas produced in the area. Riding on the success, the town of Baxiganj had now developed into a sprawling city. The jungles of Sal, Palash, and Mahua had been cut down to establish shopping complexes and offices. Our accommodation at 10, Meghmallar Street had been pulled down to make space for a flat complex in the area, thus destroying any hope of me touching base again.

Bunty, too, had fallen in love with a girl named Rosy, who danced in a club and was older than him. According to Bunty, he was attracted to her solely because Rosy was the name of the heroine in the movie Guide. His dream of playing the harmonica in the Royal Albert Hall in London didn't materialize, but he toned it down and was now preparing to play in the same club where Rosy danced. At times when he isn't courting Rosy or practising mouth organ, he still helps out Shubhom to sort out his problems in life or get even with people who mess around with him.

Acknowledgements

This is my first book or my only book that may ever reach publication stage. Hence, I have a lot of people to thank who at various stages were associated with this book.

First, my friends, Avijit, SP, Rajnish, Prasun and Ravi who are always the first persons to bear the brunt of my writing ventures, read whatever nonsense I write and yet egg me on to write further such nonsense.

Before Blue Rose stepped in, my editor Divyam who almost hand-held me to the completion of the story with all her suggestions and advice on the various aspects of the story development. Thank you, Abantika, for all your efforts in teaching me the basics of how to progress with the story. Thank you, Ritika and Shanaiya, for your suggestions in building up the story. And also, thank you Neha from Booknerds for your initial review of the story and letting me know what works and what doesn't. Thank you, Nazia, for your cover ideas that we are using in this book. I owe a special debt to my university and organizational senior Amit Agarwal, thank you for guiding me on finishing and publishing this book.

People who took time out of their busy schedule to read and review the story: S. Rangarajan, Prasad Kulkarni, Dilip Chakrabarti, Jayanta Dhar, Amit Tripathi, Piyush, Ashish Misra, Abhijit and Shailaja Hazarika and K. Whiso, thank you for your selfless efforts. Thank you, Shonali Datta, for being kind enough to share your opinion.

And lastly, thank you Blue Rose Publications for providing a platform and whatever you are doing with my story.